Contact author
Thank you for reading this book. I sincerely pray it was a blessing to you. You may leave me a note at: nancysylvester@calvarychapel.com

Please share your opinion
If you enjoyed this book (or not), I encourage you to leave a review at: www.amazon.com and www.goodreads.com

Make a difference in the lives of others
This book would make an excellent gift for anyone you know who is searching for answers or may just need reassurance, encouragement or inspiration. This book may also be used as a devotional study and group study.

Testimonial

I started reading *You're More Than Dirt* during a very fierce winter season of life. My outlook was dismal and I had little hope that the raging storms would ever pass.

It didn't take long to identify with Birdy, who was found barely coping with life at the beginning of the story. But things change as she learns to trust the Gardener with every aspect of her garden. Chapter by chapter, Birdy's relationship with the Gardener grows deeper as he teaches her life-changing truths, which always seemed to be right on time for what I was going through at that exact moment.

The lessons harvested throughout the book quickly became personal devotions, helping me better understand who our Heavenly Father really is. I learned how to listen for His voice above all others. I discovered I can sing, even at the top of my lungs, in any storm. I found that waiting on Him changes everything and that seasons do pass. He tenderly taught my bitter heart the better way and buds of hope sprang forth.

I will be eternally grateful for the deeply rooted treasures unearthed in *You're More Than Dirt*. They have changed my life and helped give me right perspective, leaving me affirmed more than ever in our Father's love.

Shanda Cobb
North Carolina, USA

You're More Than Dirt

an allegory of hope

from the Gardener

Nancy Sylvester

CCY Publishing House

CALVARY CHAPEL YORK Publishing

YOU'RE MORE THAN DIRT - an allegory of hope from the Gardener

COPYRIGHT©2018 by Nancy E. Sylvester
Published by Calvary Chapel York, York, England

Library of Congress Cataloging - in - Publication Data TXu 2-124-869

Title: YOU'RE MORE THAN DIRT - an allegory of hope from the Gardener

An allegory of abundant life as intended by our Creator. / Nancy Sylvester

1. Christian Life 2. Fiction Allegory 3. Personal Health
4. Relationship 5. Friendship

ISBN 978-1-68454-686-2

Scripture quotations: King James Version of the Bible.
Public domain.

Quote: Jonathan Edwards. Public domain.

First Printing 2020

Illustrations and cover design: Rachel Weber

Interior design and book formatting: Rachel Weber

Editing: Shanda Cobb

Printed in the United States of America by INGRAMSPARK

Dedication

To my beloved Gardener who faithfully tends my
garden with His perfect love and care

To my amazing husband who is dearest to my heart

To my precious children who I love and cherish

To my wonderful grandchildren
and joys of my life

To my wonderful parents who showed me
the Gardener

To all those who desire to meet their Gardener

Acknowledgements

With the most grateful heart, I want to thank these wonderful friends and loved ones who have each had a part in this book.

~ To my beloved David, who constantly supported me and gave me the time to write this book.

~ To my amazing children, who all played a big part encouraging me to continue to the end.

~ To Rachel and Caelen, for the hundreds of hours you invested drawing each illustration, designing the book cover and formatting over and over.

~ To my dear Charlie and Anna, who inspired me to imagine more and dream big.

~ To my precious Sarah and Dan, who supported me through all the ups and downs while writing this book.

~ To my lovely Jayne and Levi, who listened while I processed my thoughts and gave valuable input.

~ To Shanda, for your unceasing gracious, faithful, delightful attitude you displayed over the many long hours you spent Alpha-editing and revising this book, as well as all your wise counsel.

~ To Candice, for your constant encouraging care and the hours you spent Beta-reading.

~ To Sally, for being a great reinforcement from the beginning and seeing the book's potential in its infant stages.

~ To Sue, who listened and prayed for me; always encouraging me to keep going.

~ To Mary, for stretching me and being honest when I needed it.

~ To Randy, for all your editing aid and recommending this book.

~ To Megan, Laura, Andrea and Helen for your help and useful advice.

~ To Ruthie, for reading the rough draft, and cheering me on.

~ To Dan, for your reinforcement and recommendation you wrote of this book and the amazing help in publishing it.

~ To Tim, who always has an affirmative word.

~ To all my friends who prayed for me, once again I am so appreciative of each one of you.

Foreword

Do you remember a time when you found yourself approaching the end of a book only to pray it would never end? That is what happened to me when I read *You're More Than Dirt!*

When Nancy asked me to read the allegory she had written, I jumped at the opportunity. The book was so good, it drew me right back into reading it again and again! You may have heard it said that a picture is worth a thousand words. Well, God has gifted Nancy with the ability to paint word pictures worth a thousand promises. She draws you into the garden with the Gardener, Birdy, the Inspector and many others, painting the beauty of a bigger purpose that rights your thinking and soaks your heart with hope.

I found myself on an amazing spiritual journey in the garden with the Gardener. My eyes and my heart were opened by the timeless 'Keepers' saturated in Biblical truths, sowing seeds of grace and peace into my soul. This story is a field for all to glean a greater grasp of the heart of our Heavenly Father and help us better understand His mind on matters.

Many stories are written with the intention of inspiring people to believe in God and this story is no exception. If there was ever a time that this book was needed, it is now. We are living in desperately dark times and the hearts of so many are emptied of hope and filled with fear. As you dig into this story, your faith will be strengthened by the One who loves you as He teaches you to factor His absolutes into all of life's variables. This allegory leaves a big and lasting impression on the soul and will lead you onto the path of promise.

I will forever cherish this book. It has etched on my heart a deeper understanding of who God really is and who I am really created to be, leaving me revived and hope-empowered.

You're More Than Dirt is a timeless treasure and will speak into the heart of every generation. It will become one of your best-loved books and you will definitely want to pass it on to others!

Candice Beckelman
Senior Pastor's Wife
Calvary Chapel Coastlands, New Jersey, USA

Contents

CHAPTER 1

The Lawyer's Gift

Knock... Knock... Knock...

I opened one eye to peek at the clock.

"It's barely 7 a.m.!"

Knock... Knock... Knock...

"Who in their right mind would bother me this early on a Saturday morning?"

The banging went on for a while, but I didn't want to see anyone. Instead, I buried my head in my pillow and shut my eyes. Before I knew it, my sleepiness conquered the momentary interruption and rapidly lulled me into a deep slumber.

Once again, the knocker on the door clanged and jolted me awake. I glanced at the clock and realized only thirty minutes had passed.

"Who keeps knocking? Why do they feel the need to wake me up and ruin my only day to sleep in? I wish they'd leave me alone. Can't they tell I don't want to talk to them?"

I peeked out the corner of the blinds, hoping to catch a good look at the intruder. But he turned and stepped off the porch out of my view.

It definitely couldn't have been any of my friends. They left drunk in the wee hours of the morning after hanging out in the vacant lot behind my house. We built the best bonfires in that old field. Of course, it resulted in doing crazy things - like trying to jump over the flames without getting burned. We called it 'dodge the flames.' Now the only visual memories of last night's escapades were the bottles, cans, and wrappers left plastering its landscape. As far as I knew, that dumpsite didn't have an owner, at least not one that cared about it.

"Not my problem!" I mumbled to myself and headed back to bed.

Knock... Knock... Knock...

"Oh no, he's back again!"

Who might this mysterious caller be? I wonder if it's the stranger who kept knocking on my door last week? Why won't he leave me alone? My mind churned with questions.

"I didn't answer it then, and I certainly don't want to answer it now... but maybe it's someone important? Oh well, who cares?" I said, yanking the blanket over my head.

I tossed and turned until I finally dozed off into a restless dream that led me into my troubled past. The ongoing nightmare haunted me with memories of my dad yelling at my mom. In floods of tears, she would lock herself in the bathroom.

"Mommy, Mommy, are you okay?" I cried in my dream, trying to hide my five-year-old fears.

"Birdy (that's what my mother called me), I'm fine, now go in the other room," she answered, wanting to protect me from my dad's anger.

I knew that she wasn't okay, but I quickly obeyed when I heard the urgency in her voice. In search of a place to take cover, I headed towards a mound of laundry in the corner of the living room floor. 'If I could just hide under these dirty clothes,' I thought as I shrank into the middle of the pile. But that was never the case.

My dad stomped into the room and scowled, "You're next, Dirty! (He always called me Dirty instead of Birdy.)"

He reeked of alcohol, which made me even more desperate to escape the dreadful moment. My tiny body shook in terror as his wiry figure stood hunched over me. Without explanation, he brutally slapped me over and over again.

"You worthless piece of dirt! You'll never go anywhere in life! Never! Never! Never!" he shouted.

With a despicable laugh, he grabbed his coat and stormed out of the house, slamming the door behind him. Everything in me wanted to cry, but I dared not let out even a whimper. I held my breath until his car screeched out of the driveway, never to return home again.

The dark dream awakened me with a startle. My heart pounded out of control with the same old fears.

"I hate these dreams! Will they ever go away?" I shuddered as I sat up in bed and took a deep breath to calm myself.

Even though my last beating occurred years ago, the wicked memory still tormented me night after night. What did I do to deserve this punishment? Perhaps I'm the one to blame? Or maybe I'm just cursed!

'Damaged' was an understatement of how my mother and I felt after my dad left. But over time, she bounced back. She seemed to have a hidden inner strength that anchored me. That is until two years ago when she died of cancer. Part of me died with her. Now here I am, alone and numb inside, trying to find happiness in a life I never asked for in the first place.

Knock... Knock... Knock... the relentless banging began once again. Only this time, I welcomed the interruption - anything to divert the morbid residue from my nightmare.

"Okay... I'm coming!" I called as I shuffled out of bed.

I opened the door just in time to catch my visitor. There in front of me stood a medium-tall, sturdy man in a navy-blue suit. I couldn't tell his age, but I knew he was an older gentleman. He gave me a kind smile, perhaps to ease my embarrassment since I just rolled out of bed. Then handing me a thick envelope the size of a book, he gently advised that I carefully read over the material inside.

Impatient to escape the situation, I only remember him saying, "Hello... I'm the solicitor representing the case of your garden."

"What garden?" I huffed.

I didn't own a garden! What could he be talking about? He obviously noticed my blank look of utter confusion.

"Oh, the plot of land that sits at the back of your house. The good news is... I bought it for you!"

What did he mean? Was I still dreaming? Had I partied too much last night?

The lawyer attempted to make eye contact, but I refused to look him in the face. Still in my pajamas with my hair tousled in every direction, I tried to end the conversation. Not wasting another moment, I told him I'd look over the paperwork. With a quick goodbye, I abruptly shut the door before he could say another word.

"Now maybe I can get some uninterrupted sleep," I said, trying to pretend the whole thing never happened.

Why did I have to be punished with owning that ugly old field anyway? It didn't sound like good news to me. Can you imagine what everyone would say when they found out it belonged to me?

"Enough of that!" I murmured, tossing the brown envelope on my already much-needed-to-be-sorted-through stack of mail. "What a bad joke! Someone bought me a nasty chunk of dirt that will take a lifetime of work to transform! No thank you! It's not going to happen!"

I crawled back into bed, but this time, my agitated mind wouldn't allow me to fall asleep. My thoughts gravitated to the garden my mother used to take me to as a child. I'll never forget that time a man caught me picking one of his daisies. I wondered if he'd be mad as I plucked the petals off one by one and played the childish game of, 'He loves me, He loves me not.'

To my surprise, he bent down on his knees and chuckled, "My dear child, you don't need to pull off all the petals... I know what each one will say to you!"

"Wh... what w... will it say?" I stammered, afraid of his answer.

"He always loves you... and you must never forget it!" he assured with a tender smile.

I can't remember what he looked like, but I will never forget his kindness, unlike how my own dad treated us.

Months passed, and I told no one about my visit from the lawyer, nor did I open his brown envelope. Life already overwhelmed me, and I didn't need one more issue. I just wanted to live in my own reality - to eat, drink, and be merry without a care in the world. It

~"He always loves you...
and you must never forget it!"~

didn't work, though. Instead it propelled me even further into the black hole I'd created for myself.

In my endeavor to dodge the merry-go-round of confusion I called 'life,' we resumed using the field for our careless diversions. To spectators, the parties we threw gave the appearance that our lives flourished with fun. In reality, though, the illusion of happiness instantly vanished before I could grasp it. Every attempt to flee my hopelessness ended in futility. I couldn't escape this dreadful darkness - the more I tried, the emptier I became.

I had nothing.

Well, except for that plot of dirt.

Strangely, I felt connected to the property. But its exploitation tormented my thoughts with pangs of remorse. Each time I saw the pitiful land, a battle raged inside because I knew I abused it as much as everyone else. Now the guilt and shame I felt made me loathe myself even more than I already did.

"I guess I deserve to inherit that pitiful chunk of dirt! We're quite a pair - we both have no purpose... except to survive!" I mused one morning as I examined the polluted land through my bedroom window.

From early childhood, I spent all my time playing in this deserted little field. It became my kingdom, and I became its queen. As I escaped into my childish imagination, I gave each bit of rubbish a magnificent new identity. The old broken chair transformed into my throne, and the worn-out tire became my pond. Yet the reality is the plot has never been anything but pathetic dirt. What else would it be worth anyway? The lawyer said it was a garden, but that's not what I saw. Who knows, maybe he's right? Full of doubt, I shrugged my shoulders and abruptly closed the curtains.

However, day after day, the abandoned field called out, awakening a greater hope deep within that I knew must be real. Could there be any truth to the lawyer's claim? Was it more than dirt? He valued it for some reason. Maybe it contained buried treasure or something? Otherwise, why would anyone want to own it? My mind raced with questions.

Meanwhile, everything inside me rebelled against the prison of

~However, day after day, the abandoned field called out, awakening a greater hope deep within that I knew must be real.~

hopelessness I found myself in. There must be more! Thus, my search began for the answer to the 'why' behind my existence.

I started by trying to fix my world in every imaginable way. For a while, I worked extra-hard to get my ducks in a row but found the task impossible. I then set out to become a wholesome, philanthropic person, although that too left me barren. Still, the emptiness inside would not relent. As a result, I isolated myself and spiraled into a deep depression. Everyone told me to stay positive, but I possessed no power to change. My greatest achievements made me as good as the world around me - hopelessly pitiful. Desperate and unable to cope, I began to self-harm. I believed if I punished myself by cutting my arms, I would ease the internal pain or at least be distracted from the gaping wound that bled inside.

But it only made things worse.

I will never forget that freezing Friday night. I found myself in the field once again with my friends. We built a fire in the center of my new property and huddled together, hoping to stay warm. Everyone got drunk and acted like a bunch of wannabes who - just like myself - sought approval and wanted to belong. As usual, they threw their rubbish on the ground and made fun of the land's owner. Their twisted humor relished nothing more than tearing down everything around them. As I listened to their offensive remarks, my thoughts crashed into a pit of despair.

"I can't do this anymore!" I mumbled while kicking a dirt clod into the fire. "Should I just end my life? Should I? Would that solve it? Or... is there more to life than the here and now? Maybe the lawyer saw more than I can see? Could it be?"

I looked at the land around me once again and shook my head.

Disgusted and fed up with the atmosphere, I suddenly shouted, "Everyone shut up! It's my lot! I own it! And for the record, we won't be having any more parties here. It's over!"

My friends looked completely shocked and thought I was joking, but I wasn't.

Relieved that they finally knew the truth, I marched back to my house to look for the lawyer's envelope. After retrieving the large package from under a stack of papers, I quickly opened it. Inside I found a brown leather folder the size of a book. It intrigued me to say the least. I immediately sat down on the edge of my bed and began to read. I could hardly believe what I saw - every word resonated as if the author penned it specifically to me.

According to this document, the lawyer placed so much value on the garden that he willingly gave his all to buy this plot of land for me. It stated he represented me and paid every fee required by law so the garden would be freely mine. The more I studied it, the clearer it became - the document proved to be completely legal. He personally bought this field for me and wanted me to have it as my inheritance!

As I pored over the pages, my eyes began to catch sight of a new reality. The plot's potential extended far beyond what I could see. Who would've guessed that this dump started as a garden? I thought I knew every inch of its landscape, but these papers told me otherwise. The old life the field represented was not its true destiny. A whole new life awaited me there!

Completely absorbed, I read and reread each page until I lost all track of time. Before I knew it, the sun peeked through my window and warmly whispered, 'Good morning!' Indeed, it was a good morning, as well as a good night!

"Where did my night go? I need to get some sleep... but..." I deliberated, letting out a big yawn.

No way could I put this compelling document down I decided. Its loving words jumped off the pages, stirring a part of my heart I didn't even know existed. I continued to read the text, which distinctly stated the land initially began as a significant garden.

'What's the catch? What's my part in all this?' I wondered as I glanced out the window towards the field. This lawyer guy genuinely seemed to love the property. Why he bought it for me still puzzled me, though. Who was he? Where did he come from? I wished I could meet him again and ask him the many questions running through my mind. How could this parcel of land be more than worthless dirt? What destiny did he see in it that I failed to see? What made him purchase it for me? He must have seen great worth in the land, or he wouldn't have paid his all to buy it. For the first time in my life, a glimmer of hope kindled my thoughts.

"Even though it doesn't make sense to my natural mind, I still believe what this manuscript says about the land... and I want it! But what am I supposed to do now?"

Then I remembered - the pages clearly specified all I needed to do was simply receive the lawyer's gift. A garden of life or a desert of death lay before me.

"I choose life!" I resolved.

Daring to believe the truth in the document, I closed the folder and whispered, 'Thank you!' as if the kind lawyer stood right in front of me.

"I guess it is mine now!"

I took a deep breath and gratefully accepted my new lot in life. Yes, I would receive his gift, and though I didn't deserve it, my heart came alive when I believed.

"What is happening to me?"

Instantly the cold deadness melted away and a transformation birthed within that I couldn't explain. A living hope surged through my veins, flooding me with a joy I never knew existed. The dark contemplations that once troubled my soul disappeared as expectations of good restored my heart.

Could it be true that my life was *more* than dirt? Is it possible a new destiny awaited me? I wanted to pinch myself to see if I was dreaming.

"This lawyer seems to truly love me! Why else would anyone invest their whole life to buy me a garden? I matter to him! He genuinely cares about me!" I cried through tears of joy.

I now owned a garden, and *this* planted hope in my heart. And although I didn't understand why, I believed it. In that moment, the awareness of his love for me ignited my soul's candle with new life. I felt like a tiny sprout peeping through the dirt into warm sunlight.

Drowsy yet strangely happy inside, I placed the brown folder on my nightstand. After fluffing up my pillow, I closed my eyes and began to rehearse the newfound truths. Before I knew it, a peaceful rest covered me like a soft blanket, hushing my thoughts into sweet slumber.

~ Could it be true that my life was more than dirt? Is it possible a new destiny awaited me? ~

CHAPTER 2

The Gardener

I awakened with a barrel of butterflies fluttering about in my stomach - the kind a child feels on Christmas morning. My life's trajectory had changed overnight, and every anticipation ran sky-high.

"Today is the beginning of my new life! I'm not sure what it will look like... but I'm ready to find out!" I announced, jumping out of bed.

Hope resided in my heart, and I couldn't help but smile as I poured myself a second cup of coffee. After nibbling on some toast and marmalade, I opened the brown folder once more just to make sure what I read the night before was still true. Yes, the title deed to the land awaited me, and no, I didn't imagine it. Yes, it cost the lawyer all he had to buy it, so it must be valuable because nobody pays a high price for 'nothing.' Satisfied with my findings, I closed the folder, ready to venture into my new world.

"Well, Birdy... it's time to get going! Life awaits you!" I told myself as I headed out the door.

I had no idea how to create a garden, so I moseyed down to the Garden Center, hoping to pick up a few tips. They sent me home with gloves, a shovel, a rake, a hoe, a spade, and a big roll of black garbage bags. Kitted out with all the right tools, I entered my newly-acquired plot eager to embark on its true destiny.

As I inspected the land more closely, my faith quickly dimmed at the enormous task before me. Years of smashed bottles, tin cans, and who knows what else poked through the jungle of waist-deep weeds. The derelict field in no way resembled a garden except for the broken-down red brick wall and rusty iron gate. This sealed its identity as nothing but a vulnerable waste place. Oh, did I mention the old thorny pear tree that stood all alone? Its pears tasted awful - like rotten crab apples. Yes, this is what my garden looked like, and it now belonged to me!

Without any real direction, I put on my gloves and set to work.

"Hmm... where should I begin? Guess I'll start on the land closest to my house, the part that everyone can see... and then hide the rest. It looks pretty disgusting!"

My mind wrestled between the reality of what I read in the brown folder and what I saw right before my eyes.

"I suppose I shouldn't give up before I even start! I just need to keep a good attitude. Like they say, no pain... no gain!" I said, giving myself a pep talk.

It didn't take long to discover I definitely bit off more than I could chew.

I'll never forget that scorching hot day as I stood on a mound of dirt with my new shovel. I'm not sure what I struggled with most - pulling weeds or batting off the little flies that landed on my sweat-covered forehead. The tall thistles refused to let go of their squatter's rights and stubbornly fixed themselves in the ground.

"Humph... I thought I knew how to pull weeds... but even that seems impossible."

The harder I worked, the more disillusioned I became. Everywhere I turned, debris and wreckage reminded me of my dark past, representing a lifetime of hurt I longed to forget.

Rapidly losing every last bit of hope and vision, I stomped my foot on the ground and shouted, "This is *not* working... I have absolutely no idea how to build a garden by myself! What was I thinking... what am I supposed to do with this forsaken piece of dirt? Maybe I'm a fool to think this could've ever been a garden... and what's the point of all this anyway?" I cried, throwing my arms into the air.

"It's a beautiful garden..." came a voice out of nowhere.

Glancing up, I saw a medium-tall, mature gentleman wearing a plaid English flat cap. His kind face peered over the wrought iron gate, and he smiled as if he were admiring the Royal Garden. Who could this man be? Why did he wait outside when everyone else trampled through without permission? The old gate connected to two brick columns, but there were no walls on either side. Anyone could just walk in if they wanted. Yet this stranger stood respectfully awaiting an invitation to enter so as not to intrude.

"Can I help you?" I asked.

"Ma'am, it looks like you might be the one who needs help. I'm wondering if I might assist you in any way?" he replied.

I wasn't quick to respond. After all, why would anyone want to work on this landfill? He clearly didn't understand the situation!

"Are you looking for a job?"

"Yes, you might say so."

"What kind of work do you do?"

"I'm a gardener... and this is a garden!"

I glanced down and stared at the dirt. What was he talking about?

"How do you know it is?"

He hesitated for a moment and smiled. His kind eyes seemingly gazed past everything as if he recalled a happy memory from long ago.

Then looking directly at me, he said, "A gardener always recognizes a garden."

"Well, I didn't know it was a garden until I inherited it. It looks like a neglected, overgrown eyesore to me. I always wished its owner would do something about it, but I guess that's me now," I sighed, shrugging my shoulders.

"Would you like a hand to help you in any way?" he politely asked again as he started to open the gate.

"I can't pay you anything."

"Oh, it's already paid in full! I'd love to work in your garden... it looks very promising!"

I didn't have a clue what he meant. But I desperately needed a helper.

"Well... it's fine with me... if you like pulling weeds... be my guest. By the way, I suppose I should tell you my name... I'm Birdy."

"What a beautiful name! I once knew a Birdy... many years ago."

He gave me a gentle smile, although he seemed to be somewhere

~*"I'm a gardener... and this is a garden!"*~

else for a moment. As I looked into his kind eyes, the reluctance I initially felt began to disappear.

Once inside my property, he immediately took off his coat and rolled up his sleeves.

"Do you want to use my new hoe and spade?" I asked, secretly hoping he could work miracles with them.

"Thank you very much! These are the perfect tools I need!"

He eagerly set to work and appeared to be more at home on the land than I did. In no time at all, he removed more weeds than I pulled the entire morning. They effortlessly slid out of the ground - like they had no choice but to obey him. He actually seemed to enjoy the job. Meanwhile, I grunted and groaned, trying to dismantle the crabgrass I'd tackled without success.

This mysterious Gardener didn't talk much at first. But he would occasionally look up and give me an encouraging smile, almost like he knew me. He seemed thoughtful and certainly worked hard; that much I could tell. His face seemed familiar to me, yet I couldn't place where I'd seen him before. Where did this guy come from?

After slaving over the weeds all afternoon, the Gardener cleaned up the tools and put them to rest for the day.

"Are you worn out?" I asked as we walked towards the old gate.

"Oh no, it's all a delight to me!" he chuckled.

"It's not delightful to me... my muscles are not very happy... and we've only just begun!"

He put his hand on my sore shoulder and smiled, "I'll tell you what... how would you like to meet with me every morning... right here... and we'll do this together... two are better than one!"

Relieved that I wouldn't have to trudge through this alone, I welcomed his knowledgeable help and nodded a quick 'yes.'

"Okay... that settles it! I promise I'll be here waiting for you."

"What time do you want to meet tomorrow?" I asked, hoping it wouldn't be too early.

"How's 6:30 or 7:00 a.m.?" he replied, looking up to see my response.

Ugh! I hated early mornings.

"How about 8:00 a.m.?" I countered, after all, it *was* my garden.

"8:00 a.m. it is Birdy! I hope you sleep well! And thank you for allowing me to work in your garden!"

"I should thank *you*... it sure made a big difference having you here... so... I guess I'll see you tomorrow!" I bid with a glimmer of hope.

My alarm blared at 7:30 a.m. the next morning but I managed to snooze until 7:50 a.m. and made it to the garden by 8:05 a.m. No, I didn't eat breakfast, but I got there on time - well, almost on time. Frankly, I wondered if the Gardener would be there to meet me, and if so, would he be irritated I showed up late?

"Good morning! What a wonderful day, and all the better for seeing you, Birdy!" he cheerfully greeted.

His eyes sparkled as he spoke, and he seemed genuinely delighted to see me.

"Have you eaten any breakfast?"

"Uh, no... didn't have enough time!"

"Well, I brought you some!" he smiled.

He opened his thermos and poured me a big mug of freshly brewed coffee.

"Do you like cinnamon rolls? They're straight from the oven!"

"Yes, I do... wow! Thanks!"

I wasted no time taking a big, gooey bite.

"They're delicious!" I mumbled, stuffing another piece in my mouth. "The coffee is amazing as well!"

Honestly, I didn't know what to make of his goodness. People didn't do things like this without an ulterior motive, at least not in my world. Part of me couldn't help but question the legitimacy of his kindness. Why is he acting so friendly and considerate? Why did he offer to work in my garden without some form of compensation? Why did he bring me fresh coffee and the most incredible cinnamon rolls I'd ever tasted? I barely knew him! What did he want?

Little arrows of doubt bombarded my mind telling me, 'You don't deserve this charity! It's not going to last! Tell this gardener guy you're not going to go through with this, so you don't get disappointed! He's a con man! You can't trust him! Get rid of him! This whole thing is a figment of your imagination! It's all a weird fairytale, and you know there are no such things as happy endings in real life!'

I stared at the ground, struggling to sort through my suspicious thoughts and tried hard to act normal. Neither of us said a word for quite a while as we sipped our coffee.

Out of the blue, the Gardener began to hum the sweetest melody. It took me by surprise at first - a pleasant surprise I might add, because my mother used to sing the same song to me. His soft tune calmly settled the troubled thoughts churning in my mind. I studied the Gardener for a few moments, trying to figure him out. This man seemed refreshingly real and vulnerable, unlike anyone I knew. His kind eyes sparkled, leaving no place for shadows or hidden agendas. He appeared unpretentious and displayed a purity that proceeded him in all he did and said. But I still didn't know him very well. Could I trust him?

Just then, he kneeled and picked a wild daisy. Gently plucking off the petals one by one he said, "He loves you, He loves you, He loves you, He loves you, He loves you, He loves you, He loves you, He loves you, He loves you." After the last petal floated to the ground, he handed me the tiny daisy stub and said, "He loves you... and you must never forget it!"

His familiar words removed every last bit of suspicion I harbored. Who was this man? Had we met before?

"Are you ready to go over our plans for the day? I would like to hear your ideas to make sure we're on the same page," he said with a warm smile, hinting he genuinely cared.

I took another sip of coffee, buying my time because I had no idea where to begin.

"What do *you* think we should do?" I asked, looking up from my cup.

I hoped the Gardener would already have some kind of plan of attack in place.

He rubbed his chin and scanned the garden, "Well, to start... there are four kinds of soil here, so we'll have to deal with each one differently."

"What do you mean?"

"You have soil with weeds, soil with rocks, and hard soil, beaten down over the years. And of course, there is good, healthy soil as well. Each type of soil needs tender care... in order for the garden to reach its full potential," he explained.

The Gardener's eyes beamed with anticipation as he shared his ideas of how to move forward. Every word he spoke planted seeds of hope into my heart. Even though I only saw a bunch of weeds, rocks, and hard clay, he somehow saw more than lifeless dirt. And no matter how discouraged or pessimistic I felt, he continually reminded me of the beautiful life he envisioned for the garden.

"Now how does my plan of restoration sound to you?"

"Sounds good! I'll go buy the weed killer this afternoon!" I replied, adding my unsolicited two-cents.

"Oh, that's certainly one way to remove the weeds, but it fills the soil with pesticides. I have a secret way to extract them that will be healthier and more effective," he assured with a wink.

How could this guy correct me in such a gentle way? Instead of feeling torn down or ashamed, his words encouraged and empowered me. To be honest, I actually welcomed his instruction and even found myself desiring it.

"Sure, go ahead! However you want to eradicate these weeds is fine by me! You're the Gardener, and I suppose you probably do have some tricks up your sleeves. But what about all the heaps of trash and garbage everywhere?" I asked, hoping he would have an easy solution for the mountain of debris.

"It's all removable! I'm not preoccupied with any of this rubbish. None of it belongs here... it's doomed to the dumpster! And as far as

~ Even though I only saw a bunch of weeds, rocks, and hard clay, he somehow saw more than lifeless dirt. ~

the weeds go, they all have to die. We'll pull out as many as possible, then cover the ground with a non-penetrable covering so it gets no light or water. You see... if the weeds get fed in any way, they'll thrive and continue to take over the garden."

I felt a surge of hope well up inside me as I began to imagine what the garden would look like without any weeds.

"I see what you mean! Yep, all these wretched plants have to die, and I'm more than ready to bid good riddance to every last one. They represent a past I never want to see again!" I confessed.

"Here, let me pull out that big tumbleweed for you, Birdy."

In a matter of seconds, he dismantled it, roots and all.

"Look what I found hiding underneath!" he exclaimed.

"It's a massive rock! Wow, I never noticed how many there are... it looks like a rock quarry under a forest of weeds. Do we have to get rid of them as well?" I frowned, knowing it would require a lot of hard work.

The Gardener glanced at the ground and kicked one of the smaller stones off to the side.

"These rocks choke the life out of the plants and keep them from getting sunshine and air. I'm sorry, but they're not welcome here either. We must remove all that hurts and hinders this garden so it will thrive... no matter how big or heavy the boulders seem. Yes, there is a cost. But it's nothing compared to the reward," he assured, looking into my eyes to see if I understood.

"I guess you don't want anything in this garden that's not intended for it... do you?" I asked, beginning to see a bigger picture. "You're a long-term strategist, aren't you?"

~ *"It's all removable! I'm not preoccupied with any of this rubbish. None of it belongs here... it's doomed to the dumpster!"* ~

"Yes, I AM, and all my work is everlasting. We must break up the fallow ground that's been trampled on for so many years and begin anew."

"That's the story of my life! I feel like my whole existence has been one long traumatic series of hurt and pain. It's left me pretty hard in many ways. I suppose I'm skeptical and cynical about almost everything. That's not good, is it?"

"Well, you can't grow if you shut yourself off from life. We need to remove everything that keeps the seeds from thriving, especially the birds!"

"What do you mean, 'the birds'?" I asked as I set my empty coffee cup on the ground.

"Blackbirds... well, actually they're crows."

"I'm not sure what you mean... where do these crows come from?"

"I must tell you right from the beginning... you have an enemy out there who doesn't want you to have a garden. He sends in his crows to steal every seed of hope while sowing his weeds of despair. If you see any of those conniving birds, don't be afraid to shoo them out of the garden."

"Yeah, I think I saw some of those old crows today. They tried to steal my seeds of hope and sow their seeds of despair... just like you said... but they all flew away. Did *you* shoo them out?"

The Gardener didn't say anything but gave me a warm smile that put an end to every last lingering fear. He perceived the seeds of doubt and calmly addressed them, crows and all. His very presence breathed life into me, and he filled my world with hope. The genuine selfless love he displayed for my garden completely astounded me. He confidently knew the way forward, which is exactly what I needed.

"Yes, we do need to fix the soil and make it usable, and I am ready!" I resolved, not willing to settle for anything less. "There's no way I'm going to leave this garden in ruins... especially since you've shown me what it's supposed to be. I think I'm beginning to believe it may one day become a beautiful garden... well, that is if you're the Gardener!"

"I AM the Gardener!" he confirmed with a confident nod. "And if you are willing, I AM willing."

"I *am* willing... more than willing... and I'm anxious to get going. When should we start?"

But the Gardener didn't seem hurried or rushed in any way.

"Well, we've already begun, Birdy. You see, our morning appointment is an essential part of our day! Everything else flows from our time together. When we properly equip ourselves for what lies before us, we'll have a productive day."

"Does this mean we're going to do this every morning?" I questioned, hoping he would agree.

"Yes, as I promised yesterday, I will always be here waiting for you," he answered with great veracity, making me all the more eager to join him.

"It's settled then! We'll meet early every day, even if it does cost me a bit of sleep. I suppose this appointment needs to be my priority... my garden depends on it!"

"Today we laid the blueprint for every other morning. It's like plowing the first row of a field... it determines how straight the other rows line up," he explained.

"You don't know how relieved I am to start each day this way... I'm going to depend on our connection time together... I need it... and I don't think I could manage this garden any other way!"

He gently put his hand on my shoulder and gave me a warm smile. I couldn't help but return his smile. After just one morning with the Gardener, I already knew I wanted to know him more. A sweet friendship began to germinate between us. Indeed, this would become my favorite part of the day!

~ *"Everything else flows from our time together."* ~

CHAPTER 3

A New Beginning

Each morning I eagerly raced out to the garden come rain or shine. I couldn't wait to meet with the Gardener. His happy smile centered me with the confidence I needed to face the day.

Week after week, we carted wheelbarrow loads of old bottles, tin cans, and every kind of garbage you could imagine to the dumpster. With each load we discarded, I felt years of pain begin to disappear.

"Lovely to see you this morning! Are you ready for another good day?" the Gardener asked with a twinkle of delight in his eyes.

"Yes... I think I am!"

"What do you mean... 'I think I am'?"

"I mean... I know you will probably challenge me beyond my own limitations today... and I'm not sure if I'm ready for that!"

"I suppose you are right... but remember... everything I do is for your good... and you will never have to do it alone. Now, would you help me toss all these noxious weeds into the fire? I've already burned most of them."

I immediately set to work until we threw the last bunch into the blaze.

"Doesn't it feel good to watch them disappear into the flames... never to be seen again?"

"Yep! I'm glad to see them go!"

"Me too... they're the 'cursed things.'"

"They *are* cursed things!" I agreed while trying to shield my eyes from the smoke.

The flames made the already-scorching day even more unbearable. To top it off, every muscle in my body ached from the belligerent thistles we pulled the day before.

Exhausted, I scanned the mounds of untouched mess begging our attention and let out a big overwhelmed sigh.

"Are you okay?"

"Not really! We've worked so hard... but what's the point? It's an eternal battle against the weeds... and it's very discouraging!"

The Gardener saw my plight and gave me a big hopeful smile.

"Don't be discouraged... we've already won! Look at what we've accomplished over the past few weeks. The weeds and rubbish are losing ground every day! Every bit is destined to destruction... so cheer up my dear!"

I deliberated for a moment to assess the situation. The Gardener was right.

"I suppose I'm just impatient!"

"Yes Birdy... these things take time... it's all part of the process... but we'll get there!"

"I know we will... I guess I'm just weary."

"I think I know what the problem is."

The Gardener wiped his brow with his arm, reached in his backpack, and pulled out his thermos.

"Would you like a cold drink of water?"

"Thanks... I'm super thirsty! This water tastes so good... you always know just what I need!"

"My job is to keep you going!"

"Well, I sure needed that... I feel much better now... I must have been dehydrated! By the way, I didn't mean to be 'Miss Birdy Bad News'... I'm sorry about all my complaining! I know you're only trying to help me... and the garden *is* starting to take shape. I really appreciate all your hard work... I don't know what I would do without you!"

"No worries... I understand your plight and see your heart! I know it has required a lot of elbow grease... but it's all for the better! What you initially saw as foreboding drudgery, now shows great possibilities of hope. Stick with me, and we'll get there... you have my word!"

"How do you stay so cheerful and pleasant, especially in this formidable heat?"

"Do you really want to know?" he grinned. "I get to work with you! That's my happy place!"

"How can *I* be your happy place?"

"Birdy, I'm always happy when we work together! Not to change the subject... but now that we have finished here..."

"Don't tell me..."

"Yes, we get to tackle another area!"

The Gardener pointed to our next assignment - more weeds, more wreckage, more work.

"Well, here we go again... look at it... it's disgusting! I'm really sorry! How can you find a single ounce of worth in this mess?"

Without looking up from his work, he answered, "My job is to remove the filth... not expose it. Once eliminated, I will plant my new life here, and you will see what I see."

"But I still hate how I trashed it! I cringe in shame every time we discover more filth! Why would you want to work here anyway?"

The Gardener stopped weeding and rested his arm on top of his shovel as if he planned to deliver an essential, life-preserving speech.

"Birdy, you must understand that I do not identify or value this garden according to what it appears to be right now... or by what it lacks in any way. When I look at it, I only see its destiny and purpose... I will not consult your past to determine your future... you must not look at what isn't in your garden, but at what it will become now that I AM here... my business is reclamation and redemption and I won't stop until I see full transformation!"

Even though I didn't fully grasp his words, I nodded my head and got back to work.

"Why don't you put the rubbish in the wheelbarrow, and I'll pull

~ *"My job is to remove the filth...*

not expose it." ~

out the rest of these nettles," he suggested.

"Ok... that sounds good to me. I'd rather get rid of this useless junk than deal with those stinging nettles! Besides... you never know what I might find!"

I headed towards the mound of debris that included a wrecked bicycle tire, broken beach chairs, and a worn-out sneaker.

"Here's an old box... maybe I can fill it with some of this junk," I said as I lifted up the trampled cardboard.

Immediately something slithered out from underneath it.

"A SNAKE... EEEEK!" I yelled, jumping back in horror. "I HATE SNAKES! I HATE SNAKES WITH ALL MY MIGHT!"

"Where is it?" the Gardener asked, instantly picking up his shovel.

"It took off into those weeds! I hate snakes! I just hate snakes!" I screeched, feeling my heart pound in my chest.

"Oh look, it's coiled up under that tumbleweed! It's a nasty serpent, all right! He's a big one, isn't he?"

He pointed to the evil creature while beckoning me to come and see it.

"No thank you! I don't want to look at it, not even for a second! Is he poisonous?"

"Yes, he's deadly!"

"Will he bite us?"

"He would if he could, but he can't. His time is finished!"

The Gardener grinned, never taking his eyes off the vile vermin. It made me think he sincerely enjoyed the whole situation. Then in one fell swoop, he threw his shovel like a spear and chopped off the viper's head.

"You killed it! Wow! You have a perfect aim! Can you believe he lived in my garden all these years, and I didn't even know it? I would've never set foot in this place if I'd known! Weren't you afraid of him?"

The Gardener simply smiled and glanced down at the lifeless snake.

"No, I'm not afraid of him. My body holds the antidote to his poison, and he cannot hurt me. He was afraid of me, though. He knew he couldn't live in any garden that I tend. Nothing that brings fear, intimidation, or death is allowed to live in any of the gardens that I cultivate!" he declared, nodding his head in triumph.

"How did you get the antidote?"

"Oh, many years ago a serpent bit me a on the heel of my foot... but he didn't realize I'd crush his head in the process."

The Gardener picked the snake up by its tail, and without a word, threw it into the blazing fire to incinerate with the weeds.

"Thank goodness you were here! You're undaunted by anything in this garden! You have no idea how relieved this makes me feel! I couldn't have coped by myself. Honestly, I'm so ready for a new beginning... I just want to get rid of every last bit of the past!" I declared, throwing my hands up in full surrender.

Before the Gardener could respond, an unexpected crack of lightning flashed before our eyes. A welcome breeze and much-

~"Nothing that brings fear, intimidation, or death is allowed to live in any of the gardens that I cultivate!"~

needed summer rain followed close behind. Now when I say rain, I mean rain! It came on so suddenly, neither one of us had time to seek shelter.

"This is a good rain! Don't be afraid to let it completely soak you and wash off all the dirt," he assured as we both stood laughing underneath the heavenly rinse.

I raised my hands to the sky and let the cool water stream down my body, leaving a big pool at my feet. The delightful moment marked a new beginning I would never forget.

"You know... this 'happy rain' has removed the 'old' so that the garden can begin anew," the Gardener affirmed.

"Yes, it's washed away the haunting memories of my old life... I feel as free as a little bird now!"

"Wonderful! That's what I came to do! Birdy, we have so much to look forward to! Do you see how the rain softened the soil to prepare it for its new life?"

As quickly as the thundershower appeared, it passed. The sun poked his head through the clouds and greeted us with a magnificent rainbow. Its colors spanned the entire sky with a promise of hope. Before long, every cloud disappeared, and the air swirled with the fragrance of wet soil. The delicious smell made me want to kiss the ground.

"The garden is now ready for a fresh beginning, and so am I!" I announced, feeling incredibly light and joyful.

Excited about the future, I resolved to watch the Gardener and carefully follow his every instruction. He taught me with such

42

kindness and understanding. Even when I didn't get things right the first time, he would patiently persevere with me. He'd simply say, 'Mistakes are part of growing... I will teach you how to succeed in whatever I ask you to do... never be afraid to ask for my help... because I can always fix it. Remember... I can hear you from every place in your garden... and I'll always answer.'

"Are you hungry?" the Gardener asked, interrupting my thoughts. "Here's a nice dry spot under this tree. Let me lay out my blanket so you can have a seat. Are you ready for some lunch?"

"I'm starving... how'd you know?"

He handed me a nice chunky sandwich neatly wrapped in brown paper.

"This looks delicious... what kind is it?"

"Taste and see... I know you will like it!"

"I'm sure I will! How do you always know what I like?"

The Gardener didn't answer my question. Instead he offered me cup of cold water with a thin slice of lemon.

"Now, Birdy, would you like to tell me what's really on your mind?"

He seemed to know my thoughts before I did, but I decided to tell him anyway.

"I was thinking about you!"

"And...?"

"You take such good care of this garden and understand me so well. Even when I'm overwhelmed and try to hide my feelings, you encourage me with just the right words."

"It's my responsibility to tend to this garden, which means that nothing gets neglected... including you!"

"Well, what's my job?"

"Just follow me... I'll lead you every step of the way!"

"That seems doable... simply follow your lead... that's all?"

"Yep, that's all!"

His words comforted me and set my mind even more at peace. Something about his unrelenting kindness fostered my desire for his continual company. And in spite of my earlier suspicions about him, I began to consider him my trustworthy friend.

"You know... I've really enjoyed getting to know you... and I've actually found myself looking for opportunities to chat throughout the day. It almost seems like the more we communicate, the more this plot is beginning to resemble a garden!"

"This my dear, is the key to the garden's growth! The transformation in this garden is a product of the sweet relationship that is growing between us."

"That's why we need to stop and connect!"

"Yes, these times are often more important than the actual work we do."

"I agree... I could listen to you all day long! Your truth feeds me with rich understanding! When you share your vision for the garden's future, I feel like a child looking into a candy shop window... longing to get a glimpse into your unseen world. You see beyond the 'now' into a sweeter, more abundant, much greater reality, that is more real than what I can comprehend. For the first time in my life, I'm beginning to see I have a reason to live and a destiny to fulfill... one that is outside anything this world could offer! It's so magnificent! Oh... if only I could see as you do!"

"You will... there is always more than meets the eye... and I will teach you how to see it!" he assured with a wink and a smile. "By the way... I see you liked your avocado and tomato sandwich!"

"I did... thanks... I devoured it! Any crumbs left on the blanket must be yours... because I ate every bit of mine!"

"Good, this will keep you going for a while!"

"I have loved our picnics together... they're like a banquet to me!"

"Why's that?"

The Gardener raised his eyebrows and grinned, ready to enjoy my answer.

"Well... aside from all the great food... I love to sit and laugh about the funny moments in our day! Your sense of humor is the best medicine for me! Then of course... there are those times when you patiently listen as I disclose my restless heart to you... and with one gentle word, you still my thoughts with hope and peace."

"Yes... I too cherish these times!"

We both sat silent for a moment and reflected on our many

delightful conversations. Before I knew it, my imagination floated away like a hot air balloon as I envisioned this new life he described. After a few minutes, the Gardener put his hand on my shoulder and gently brought my balloon down to earth.

"I think it is time for us to get back to work!" he said as he shook out his plaid blanket and folded it up.

"As you say, Sir Gardener!"

Energized and ready to tackle the afternoon, I put my gloves back on to avoid getting dirt under my nails. Unlike the Gardener, who preferred to use his bare hands and seemed to enjoy running his naked fingers through the soil as if it were alive.

"Follow me," he said, picking up his axe. "We have a job to do."

"What job is that?"

"We need to prune back the pear tree. See those wild branches? They're full of disease... and we're going to chop them off! The old life has to die so it can thrive with new life!"

The Gardener smiled, revealing he had great hope for the old tree.

"So basically, you're making the bad tree into a good tree... am I right?"

"Absolutely... that's what I do! When I make a tree good, the fruit will be good! Watch this!" he chuckled as he swung his axe.

In a matter of minutes, he chopped the tree right down to the stump. Meanwhile, I cleaned up the old dead limbs sprawled all over the ground.

"Be careful! They're mean-spirited boughs. Their spiky thorns are angry at their demise... they'll assault anyone who comes near them," he warned.

"Ouch! They certainly are! This thorn just attacked me... look, it poked right through my glove and stabbed my hand!"

I quickly removed my glove to clean the blood off my fingers.

"Let's have a look." The Gardener took my hand in his and inspected the wound, "It's a pretty big gouge."

He held the cut together with his fingers and wrapped his handkerchief around it.

"These gloves are useless... they didn't protect me at all!"

"You're right... all your self-effort will never be able to protect you from the weeds... you need more than that," he said as if he alone knew the remedy.

I never examined the Gardener's hands up close until that moment. As he tended to my puncture, I noticed deep scars in the center of both his palms. How did I not see them before? It must have been extremely painful when it happened. Were his wounds the consequence of removing the filth in my garden? I tried hard not to stare, but I couldn't take my eyes off of his hands.

"I hate those cursed thorns... I know what it feels like to have them pierce you," he softly said, bringing me back into the moment.

"Ha... have you been pierced by thorns also?" I stammered, a bit afraid of the answer.

"I have... would you like to see where?"

"Yeees..." I slowly answered, overwhelmed at the possibility that my garden might be the culprit of his dreadful injuries.

He then held out his hands and showed me his wounds. In the center of his palms lay horrific marks on this man who let my garden scar him for life. Overcome and undone by his great love for me, I felt a warm tear roll down my cheek. What had my garden done to him?

Unable to speak, I hid my face in my hands and began to weep uncontrollably. Those piercings proved once and for all how much the Gardener loved me.

I would never forget what I saw that day. No, I didn't fully understand the pain he suffered. But I comprehended enough to appreciate how much his love for me and my garden cost him. I knew right then I could trust his love forever.

He gently took my hand in his and kissed the bound-up wound. Instantly all the pain disappeared.

"My hand doesn't hurt anymore! What happened? What did you do?"

I carefully pulled the handkerchief back to see why my injury suddenly felt better.

"Look, it's all gone! It's like it never happened!"

Completely astonished, I showed the Gardener my healed hand.

He let out a delighted laugh.

"Wonderful!" Tenderly gazing into my eyes, he then said, "I noticed your other scars as well."

"Oh, no!" I shrank back in shame.

The Gardener must have seen all the self-inflicted marks lacing my arms from my past. I quickly tried to cover them up, but when I examined my arms, they were no longer there! I couldn't find a trace of them!

"Th... they're gone! What... what is happening to me? You... you did this for me! You did this! How? Why? Thank you... thank you!"

Tears of joy streamed down my cheeks. I felt the Gardener's wounded hands gently lift my chin to meet his face. His eyes beamed with utter compassion.

With a reassuring smile, he softly said, "Only I AM to bear the scars from the damage done to this garden."

"But you don't deserve it! I made this mess. It's all my doing!"

"I wanted to do it, Birdy," he whispered, "and I would do it again for you!"

I was whole!

~ *"Only I AM to bear the scars from the damage done to this garden."* ~

CHAPTER 4

Sweet Surrender

"I love springtime!" I cheerfully announced upon entering the garden.

My ears perked up to the sweet familiar sound of my favorite Gardener singing my favorite song. Enchanted by the joyful music, I let it lead me to his whereabouts. I found him serenading a little sprout as he gave it a drink of fresh water.

"Good morning! What has inspired your melody so early this lovely day?"

"Oh, this old tune? I always sing it to the plants!" he chuckled through a sparkling grin.

"Hmm... singing to the plants?"

"Why yes, I sing over all my creations! Did you know it inspires them to grow? Besides, I can't help but sing when I am happy."

"You sure love what you do, don't you?"

"I love to bring beauty out of ashes... and a garden out of dirt! I love to give hope, and I especially love to create new life!"

The twinkle in his eye affirmed how much pleasure he received cultivating the garden. He nurtured each individual flower with such attentiveness and knew the names of all the plants - from the largest to the tiniest sprouts. He gave each one significance. Every part of the garden mattered to him.

"Do you know you're a very good Gardener? I'm just sorry that my garden's so small!"

The Gardener stopped watering for a moment and looked into my eyes.

"Birdy... I don't need more... I just need all."

~ "Birdy... I don't need more...

I just need all."~

"I guess that's true... the more stones and weeds you remove... the bigger the garden becomes. It actually appears larger than when we started. Only *you* could take an unimportant measly plot of land and make the most of every inch of its soil! Your vision is beyond anything that I could ask, think, or even imagine. How do you do it?"

He put his hand on my shoulder, "I'll explain later! Not to change the subject, but... do you have a moment? I have something I'd like to show you. Will you follow me?"

"Yes! Where are we going?" I inquired, trailing close behind him.

"I'd like to see what you think of my latest handiwork."

He guided me to the right-hand corner of the garden where he'd removed an old overgrown bush. In the clearing sat two white wooden Adirondack chairs perched in a wonderland of bluebells. In between the chairs stood a weathered antique birdbath which the Gardener found tipped over and covered with moss. Now carefully restored, it brimmed with water, ready to welcome its first visitors.

"Come have a seat!" the Gardener beckoned.

"This is comfortable to sit in!" I said as I leaned back in the Adirondack chair next to him. "Oh my goodness! Do you see all the bird feeders hanging in the branches above us? There must be dozens of them... where did they come from? Did you do all this? It's... well... it's incredible!"

Before he could answer, a host of birds suddenly greeted us, flocking in to feed and bathe. They fluttered about everywhere. The whimsical moment exceeded my most imaginative dreams.

"Look at all these birds! I've never seen so many different kinds in one place!"

"Yes... notice there are hummingbirds, wrens, robins, purple martins, swallows, red cardinals, blue jays, doves, sparrows, finches, and many more!"

"Wow! Look at them frolic in their new bird sanctuary... you can tell they love it!"

We sat quietly for a few minutes and listened to the birds perform their glorious symphony. Then out of nowhere, they began to land on our arms. One even perched on my head! The scene reminded me of something out of a fairytale.

"What do you think of all of this?" the Gardener asked with anticipation.

He studied me like a parent watching his child unwrap the first gift on Christmas morning. I could see he delighted in my delight as I laughed in wonder.

"This is amazing! You are amazing! How did you know I love birds? I'm sure I never mentioned it before!"

"Well, *Birdy*..." he grinned. "I think your name gave it away!"

"You're probably right. I guess I can't hide it very well, can I now? I think all your creations are intricately designed just for me. You spoil me!"

"I'm not sure if I spoil you, but I do cherish you!"

"Well, if you want my opinion... it's perfect! It reveals the work of a perfect creator!"

The more I observed the Gardener, the more I realized he made perfect choices in everything he did. But he liked to communicate with me before he did anything of major importance, as if I were in charge. I suppose the garden did belong to me, although I had no real vision, at least none worth implementing. My feeble ideas paled in comparison to his plans, and my efforts were useless apart from him. Whenever I tried to fix the garden by myself, it always turned into a big mess. Like when I decided to surprise the Gardener and bought an old used lawnmower. I thought I got it for such a good deal. Unfortunately, its deafening motor disrupted the peace in the garden - not to mention it quit working after the first five minutes! We ended up taking the old thing back and bought a new, quieter one. And I'll never forget the time I thought I'd help the Gardener and buy 'special' plant food. Well, let's just say, it took him a while to nurse all those plants back to life after I administered it to their little roots. He taught me the best supplement was his very own blood meal he personally prepared for my garden. It not only infused the soil with life-giving nutrients, but it also protected it from other pests. Of course, he spared nothing but his very best to cover the entire garden. As a result, it flourished under his care. Even with all my 'well-meaning' blunders, he never made me feel bad. Instead, he gently showed me a better way. All of this confirmed the time had come to turn the entire garden over to him.

"Birdy, what are you thinking about?" he tenderly asked, placing his hand on mine.

"You, my dear Gardener... and... well..." my voice trailed off, still deep in thought.

"Remember, I AM the Gardener, and I make it my business to know everything that goes on in this garden. So... do you want to tell me what you were thinking about? Or should I tell you?" he chuckled.

"Well... I can't help but notice how everything you do is birthed out of so much love. Your love continually chooses me, honors me, treasures me, and provides everything I need to flourish. Just look at how this garden thrives!"

He gave me a nod and grinned.

"And you know... I've been thinking... why don't you build yourself a small cabin on the property? After all, when I arrive at the garden every morning... you're always here and I don't think I've ever seen you leave when evening comes. When do you go home? Do you ever leave?"

"Well, someone needs to be here to protect it!" the Gardener said, raising his eyebrows. "Not to mention, there's always work to be done!"

"You love my garden so much more than I do! It's like a child to you, isn't it?" I replied with a big smile. "As I look back on the past months, I can honestly say, I haven't worried about anything. You accomplish so much around here that I am not even aware of... and at end of the day... I can unequivocally say you're the best thing that ever happened to this garden. You know... as our friendship has grown... my trust in you has also grown... I'm beginning to trust you

~"Remember, I AM the Gardener, and I make it my business to know everything that goes on in this garden."~

more than I trust myself. And... well... would you mind if I officially commit the garden to you and put you in charge of all the decisions? It would take a big burden off of me. Besides, you always go before me with *your* perfect plans, *your* perfect provision, and *your* perfect perspective. Honestly... you take care of every need that arises. So here is my proposition.... will you please take full ownership of my garden and do with it as you wish?"

I hesitated for a moment as I thought about all the logistics required to transfer the garden into the Gardener's name.

"Hmm... but I'm just not sure how I can legally give it to you."

Just then, a vague memory of the lawyer flashed across my mind. Could he help? How would I find him after all this time? Where would I start looking?

"Remember the lawyer I told you about... the one who paid everything he had to give me this garden?"

"Yeees..." he slowly nodded, waiting for me to continue.

"I should've taken time to get to know him that day when he delivered the title deed to my garden. He seemed like such a nice man... you know, he might be the right person to consult about putting the garden in your name... but I'm not sure where to find him now... I should have stayed in touch with him."

"It may not be as hard as you think. What do you recall most about him?"

As I sat there trying to remember that eventful morning, it slowly began to come back to me.

"He was sure persistent about meeting you that day," the Gardener added as if he too were there.

How did he remember that morning when I barely remembered it myself?

"Birdy..." the Gardener gently, but firmly called my name.

In a moment of realization, I blurted out, "The Lawyer... had a strong but gentle voice... a lot like yours... in fact... it... it sounded... very similar... well... actually, *identical* to yours! Wait..."

The veil that kept me from fully knowing my Gardener and seeing what he accomplished for me instantly ripped from top to bottom.

"It was you! It was you! It was you that day, wasn't it? You're not only my Gardener... you're the Lawyer that bought my garden for me, aren't you! *You* made it possible for me to have a garden and a Gardener!"

He nodded and gave me a pleased smile, assuring me he indeed *was* the Lawyer.

"*You* already paid for every bit of this garden... so *you* should make all the decisions from now on. Here... take the key to the gate! It's all yours! You're its rightful owner!"

"Thank you! I'll make sure the gate is unlocked for you every morning... I promise... and you will always find me here waiting for you... you have my word."

He winked and gave me a big grin as he put the key safely in his shirt pocket.

"I do have a question I've always wondered about..."

"What is that, my dear?"

"Well... why did you pay all you had to buy this garden? What did you see in it that would make you do that? I suppose that is two questions," I chuckled.

The Gardener tenderly spoke, "My child... I found a treasure here, so I gave my everything to buy it."

"Seriously? Where is this great treasure? I want to see it!"

Without another word, he put his hand on my shoulder and looked directly into my eyes. His face beamed as if he couldn't wait to tell me the secret of his newly-found treasure.

"It's you, my dear Birdy! Yes... it's you," he whispered with a pleased smile as if he discovered the greatest treasure on earth. "I gave my very life to buy this garden so that it would bloom in full splendor. You see, I understand its priceless value and will not stand still until I unearth every bit of its treasure."

Now everything started to make sense to me. My Gardener - the Lawyer - understood the garden's true worth. He would not stop working until it came into its full legacy!

Overwhelmed and moved by his unconditional love for me, I whispered back, "Of course, you should have full reign over the entire garden! Will you please restore it into what you destined it to be? It's an easy decision for me. I know I can completely trust your capability... and it's far beyond what I can see, understand, or even dream!"

Before the Gardener could respond, a sparrow landed on his finger. The little bird sat fearless and bold, almost as if this special friendship occurred daily. He then began to tweet like he expected something.

"Would you like a cuddle?" the Gardener asked, reading the bird's mind.

He kissed the top of the little fellow's head and stroked the back of his neck.

"You know, Birdy, not one sparrow falls to the ground without my awareness or concern."

I watched in awe as he carefully inspected the tiny being. Our new friend rested a few more moments on the Gardener's finger before he fluttered away.

"No one compares to you... or is more qualified to do the things you do. How could I *not* entrust my garden to you? Your presence is what makes it a true paradise! From now on, the garden must be identified by your name alone... I can now confidently say I'm *your* Birdy!"

"You are my Birdy!" the Gardener agreed, stroking the top of my head just like he did to the little sparrow.

For the first time in my life, I felt completely secure and at rest. A perfect peace enveloped me like never before.

The Gardener and I reclined in our chairs drinking in the afternoon sun. But that didn't last long before we were sprayed by the blue jays recklessly splashing about in the birdbath.

"I guess they wanted us to enjoy the water as well!" the Gardener laughed.

"Look at them! They don't have a care in the world! I feel like I could

jump right in and join them!"

"I'm not sure if there's enough room for that!"

We both giggled at the thought as we wiped the water off our faces.

"I can't help but notice how they play without a care... free from all life's worries. I feel like one of those birds today... happy and free. I love the life that you've created for me here!"

The Gardener took my hand in his and whispered, "*Surrender* is a pleasant resting place... isn't it?"

Before I could answer, a snowy white dove landed on my left shoulder and began to coo. Neither of us dared speak as we sat in reverent awe soaking in the dove's presence. After a few moments, the lovely creature gently took flight, leaving behind a heavenly peace. Speechless by the wonder of it all, the Gardener and I basked in the glowing love and joy that lingered.

"Do you know why the dove landed on your shoulder?"

I wasn't sure, but he went on to answer his own question.

"He found a resting place. He sensed your quiet heart and knew you would freely welcome and receive him, so he graced you with his presence."

"A wonderful presence!" I wholeheartedly agreed.

What a beautiful surrender.

The Gardener had my all!

Full surrender and full peace!

~ "Surrender is a pleasant
resting place... isn't it?" ~

CHAPTER 5

The Secret Place

"Ugh! What a horrific dream!" I groaned as I sat up in bed.

I felt worn out after being chased all night by an invisible villain determined to destroy me with his armory of unseen weapons.

"Enough of that!" I resolved, trying to shake off the fears left by my nightmare. "Hopefully today will be better than last night!"

I looked out the window to see what the sky decided to deliver. To my dismay, dark, ominous clouds loomed on the horizon, which seemed to be an appropriate depiction of my gloomy mood.

"Yuck! Look at this nasty weather... maybe I should just stay in bed... but... I know the Gardener's expecting me... and I don't want any more bad dreams."

After finishing my oatmeal, I dutifully dressed in my warmest clothes and headed out to the garden. When I opened the door, a blanket of dense fog greeted me, sending a damp chill through my body.

"Oh no... look at this fog... what's the point of working in a garden I can't even see?"

I got as far as the gate and heard what sounded like a pack of snarling wolves. The eerie atmosphere quickly convinced me to head back to my warm bed.

"Hello, Birdy!" greeted the Gardener's cheery voice, stopping me in my tracks.

"Where are you?"

"Right here... beside you... we need to get you into a safe place where you are shielded!"

He put his arm around my back and carefully shepherded me into the garden, closing the gate behind us.

"Did you hear those wolves? I don't know how many there were... I couldn't see them in this horrific fog... their growls made me want to run for my life."

"Yes... I heard them too... but rest assured, they cannot enter this garden! Now, let's start over, Birdy... and good morning to you!"

"*Is* it a good morning?"

It didn't appear to be, and I secretly hoped the Gardener would answer, 'No, it's not; let's cancel the day in the garden.' Not that I didn't love him, but I really didn't feel like wrestling in the fog all day long.

Instead, he hugged me and said, "Oh, every day is a good day! Here, take my hand, I have a surprise to show you. Do you trust me even when you can't see me?"

I thought I trusted him, but today I battled to trust in anything I couldn't see.

The Gardener put out his hand again and gently repeated, "Do you trust me?"

I avoided his question and replied, "Well, I guess I'll need to hold onto you because there's no way I'll be able to keep up if I can't even see you."

Without a word, he carefully clutched my hand and led me through a winding path to the garden's farthest corner. There, under an apple tree, he pointed to his surprise.

"Wait... do I see a swing?" I asked, only able to make out an outline amidst the thick wall of fog before me.

"Come closer!" he bid. "Do you see it now?"

As I drew nearer, it became clear.

"It's a swing for two with a canopy over it! I've always wanted one... how did you know? I don't think I ever mentioned it to anyone! Wow... I love it... thank you!" I exclaimed, feeling my mood lighten a bit.

The Gardener sat down on the swing and motioned me to join him, so I obediently followed his lead. Neither of us spoke a word for a while as we floated back and forth through the mist. His calm presence began to melt away the commotion I felt inside.

"Do you like my surprise?" he softly asked, breaking the silence.

"Of course, I do! It's wonderful!"

"Let's call this our 'secret place' where we are free from all of life's hustle and bustle. Here, you have my full attention... and everything else can wait while we share this time together. Now... are you going to tell me what's been bothering you all morning?"

"How could you tell I was bothered?" I asked, trying to buy time while I assessed my own feelings.

The Gardener slowed the swing down, looked into my eyes and said, "You know Birdy... this garden has no hiding place in it... and it's safe to tell all."

"Well... truth is... I don't like fog... and I don't like any kind of wolves... especially creepy ones that lurk about in the dark... and... I don't like wrestling with the things I can't see."

"Do you know that nothing in this garden is invisible to my eyes? Even the darkness is not dark to me. Would you like to know the key to overcoming dark, fearful, foggy days like today?" He put his arm around me, nestled me even closer to himself and whispered, "Don't wrestle with what you can't see... just nestle close to me... and *trust me*. Simply rest with me... even in the heaviest fog!"

"Nestle... don't wrestle! Is that all I need to do when I can't see?"

"Yes... I AM your safe place... and when you're with me, these fears cannot remain. Nestle, don't wrestle... you must never forget that I will always be waiting for you in our secret place... it is here that you will gain true perspective and peace. Even though this mist may temporarily annoy you, it actually waters the plants in this garden. The tiny droplets condense on each leaf until they run down the stalks and soak the roots. The fog does not remove the goodness in your garden... it only hides it."

"Hmm... I suppose it's much ado about nothing! But what about the wolves?"

"There will always be wolves, but they can only prowl outside the garden!"

"That's a relief... you don't know how comforting your words are... I feel like a little lamb safe in the arms of my shepherd. Your love quiets my spirit and centers my soul with fresh hope. Why did I become so fearful? How did I let a little bit of water or those mysterious growls

~ *"Nestle, don't wrestle...*

you must never forget that I will always

be waiting for you in our secret place...

it is here that you will gain

true perspective and peace." ~

intimidate me... what if I'd gone back to bed? I probably would've ended up with more nightmares."

"More nightmares?"

"Yes... I had horrible dreams all night long of an invisible enemy trying to destroy me!"

"You do have an invisible enemy who is a liar and a thief... but he is not going to steal this day! Remember... when you are with me, you never have to be afraid or intimidated by anything you can't see."

I knew he was right. As we lingered on the swing, the Gardener revealed his heart more deeply than I had previously known. He knew no guile - only beautiful simplicity that fulfilled my heart's desires. As I took the time to listen and observe him, I found myself growing to love him more and more. Like two best friends, we relished each moment together.

"I wish we could do this all the time," I longingly sighed.

"We can... a lifetime of my love awaits you in this secret place."

"I look forward to every second... there is so much more... and I feel like I'm only able to see one ray of sunlight while the whole sun awaits my discovery."

The Gardener simply smiled as if he designed it this way. Maybe he knew I wouldn't be able to handle the entirety of his goodness all at once.

"The day has sure flown by... hasn't it? I didn't even notice it got dark until now."

"This happens when we pour our hearts out to each other... we become unaware of the trivialities of the day. There is something else I don't think you noticed..."

"What's that?" I responded, not sure what the Gardener meant.

"See all the stars out tonight?"

When I surveyed the sky, I realized the fog had dissipated.

"The fog is gone! It's all gone! When did it leave? How did I not spot it until this very moment?"

"You didn't observe it because you were busy using your other senses. Sometimes we think we need to use all five senses to exist, but you have a much greater sense that is deep within you. This sense sees and hears beyond your eyes and ears. You used that sense today," the Gardener explained.

"I suppose there is a whole other world I can't see with my natural eyes... isn't there? How do I tap into that reality?" I asked, trying to process what he was saying.

"Be still and listen. In the quietness, where everything else is tuned out, you will recognize my voice above all... and hear me speak of things so precious that only your heart will understand."

I realized right then how much he longed for me to live in this sacred secret place.

"Hmm... is this what nestling is? I wouldn't trade it for anything in the whole world!" I said, leaning in closer to him.

As the evening drew near, all quieted into silence and only the sound of a nightingale could be heard singing in the distance.

"Can you see the moon anywhere?" I whispered.

"It's over there in the eastern sky... do you see that tiny glowing sliver?"

"Oh, I see it... I guess the moon left its job of lighting up the evening skies to the Milky Way!"

"Look how many stars are out, Birdy! These extra dark nights enable us to see them even more clearly!" he replied as he carefully pointed out the various constellations. "Do you know that all creation

~"*Be still and listen. In the quietness, where everything else is tuned out, you will recognize my voice above all… and hear me speak of things so precious that only your heart will understand.*"~

continually speaks life and truth to those who have ears to hear?"

As I listened to him, I discovered incredible details that, for many, would seem random and unimportant, but to me, they spoke of another reality. His knowledge and profound understanding of nature intrigued me. And as he explained the 'why' behind every part of creation, it all made sense - right down to the very last star. At that moment, I realized its intended destiny ever-declared its maker's glory.

"You're right! When I see how you have deliberately orchestrated every detail in my garden... I'm amazed! It reveals the loving hand of a creator who cares about even the tiniest intricacy. The *more* I see your meticulous work, the *more* I'm aware of your love."

"Speaking of *more*, I have *more* to show you... or are you getting tired?"

"I've lost all sense of time... I suppose it is getting a bit late... but I *do* love your detours... they're little adventures that always end with happy memories!"

"Okay... it won't take too long... and you won't be disappointed... I promise!"

"It's quite dark out there... do you think we'll need a flashlight?"

"Remember, I know this garden like the back of my hand... I'm its creator!"

"Of course you are... like you said, the darkness is never dark to you. You always see the unseen... and when I live in your unseen realm, I no longer need to fear any other invisible foes... do I?"

"You're absolutely right!"

The Gardener took my hand in his, and we set out on what felt like a jungle expedition. The garden lay completely still except for the crickets chiming their evening melodies. I followed close behind him as we weaved our way through the tropical paradise.

"Be careful!" he warned.

We stepped off the beaten path for a moment into the lush vegetation. He loved to take seemingly risky shortcuts, making me fully rely on him every step of the way. With a sudden stop, he knelt down and lifted up a big leaf from an Elephant Ear plant. I watched with curiosity as he exposed a large rock hidden underneath.

"Look at this, Birdy! It's a secret you won't find in the daytime!"

His voice resonated with excitement like he discovered a long-lost fortune.

"What is it?" I asked, leaning in to get a closer look.

There in front of us lay a whole nest of glowworms. I'd never seen anything quite like it. Hundreds of them wiggled about, lighting up the rock.

"It's fantastic! How did you find them? How did they get there?"

"This is what I do! Like I said before, I make it my business to know everything in this garden. How do you think these little fellas got on this rock in the first place? These surprises are our treasures in the nighttime. But there is *more* I want to show you... follow me!"

He helped me to my feet before leading me through what seemed like a thick forest of pine trees and ferns.

"Okay... are you ready?" the Gardener asked as we rounded the garden's back corner.

Instantly a host of fireflies sparkled around us. They whirled and danced about, entertaining us with the most spectacular display of fireworks. The Gardener and I stood speechless, fully captivated by their brilliant light show. His face beamed with utter pleasure.

"Do you like it?" the Gardener whispered, anticipating my response.

"I do! I do!" I quietly answered, fully enthralled.

"These are the wonders in the night, hidden for those who will trust me to lead them through unknown territory in the darkest of times... even in the fog," he softly assured.

"I'm amazed... I had no idea about any of this!" I said, finally finding my words. "Thank you for taking me by the hand and leading me through this foggy day and pitch-black night. I would have never seen these miracles otherwise. Thank you for showing me how to trust you! Thank you for helping me to see past the fog! Thank you for the swing! Thank you for teaching me to nestle... not wrestle! Thank you for taking me into our secret place! Thank you for the adventure of a lifetime! Thank you for all the hard work you do in this garden! Thank you for being my best friend! Thank you... thank you!"

The Gardener gave me a gentle squeeze and said, "I think it's time to take you back to your house. You need to get rested up for tomorrow."

Like a satisfied newborn nestled against her mother's breast, I let out a peaceful sigh as he held me for a moment or two.

"Would you like to meet in our secret place every day?" he asked, lowering his voice as if he didn't want to wake the rest of the garden.

"I'd love to! You know my greatest joy is to be with you... and the thought of being apart from you is my greatest dread. Your presence is my transformation... where your good... has become my good! Can you see why I just want to be with you?"

"Well, I'll never leave you... not ever!" he promised.

"What more could I want? I'm ruined for everything but your dear presence!"

I let out a big, contented yawn.

"It's time for you to go to sleep, my little one. Only sweet dreams for you tonight!" he assured, gently tapping the end of my nose.

"Goodnight, my dear Gardener!" I faintly whispered.

"Goodnight!" he bid ever-so-softly, kissing me on the top of my head.

His peace filled the garden.

He gave his beloved sleep.

~ "I'm ruined for everything but your dear presence!" ~

CHAPTER 6

Re-creation

Once upon a time, I loathed mornings - but not anymore! The bright sunlight streamed through my bedroom window, reminding me of the Gardener's daily charge, 'Birdy, every day is a celebration in this garden... enjoy the celebration!'

"That's exactly what I am going to do today!" I resolved with a nod.

Excited to see the Gardener, I threw on my clothes, ran a brush through my hair, and raced out to the garden. What rare flowers would he plant? Which bushes or trees would he resurrect? He knew exactly where to place each seedling, and I couldn't wait to discover his latest designs.

"Good morning, Master Gardener! Good morning! Master Gardener?"

After no reply, I set out to look for him, only to hear sweet whistling faintly in the distance.

"I can hear you... but I can't see you," I said as I followed the happy melody.

I finally found him in full conversation with the birds.

"Good morning, my dear Birdy!" he greeted with a big smile.

"And, good morning to you, my dear Gardener! What are you doing over here?"

"Oh... I'm thinning out the ivy... so it doesn't take over the garden wall. Now, how might you be today?"

"I'm doing great! I woke up this morning and decided to celebrate life!"

"Good! There is much to celebrate... but right now would you mind celebrating while you help me finish this last bit of work? We need to remove some of this ivy to make room for the climbing roses."

"Do you remember when this wall was an old pile of bricks? Now look at it!"

Along its borders were yellow and purple pansies, snapdragons, marigolds, and the most delicious lavender you could ever smell. The purple wisteria hung like Chantilly lace on the canopy of white trusses the Gardener built nearby. Every single flower he cultivated expressed its own unique beauty, altogether creating a plethora of colorful life. He gleaned from a world of flora past my comprehension, planting rare species I never knew existed like Pelican flowers, Mandevillas, and Angel Trumpets.

"How do you know where to place each flower?"

"Oh, I've made this garden glorious... just like my own! You see, I'm re-creating it into what I first intended it to be!"

"Wait, what do you mean? Are you saying you're restoring its original destiny by creating my garden to look like your *own* garden?" I asked, trying to process what he just said.

The Gardener smiled from ear to ear and answered, "Your conclusion is correct, my dear!"

A new world of understanding burst open before me.

"No wonder you saw its value when everyone else saw dirt! No wonder your vision has never faltered, and you know exactly what to do and when to do it... no wonder the weeds obey your commands and must be removed... no wonder all the plants flourish under your care... no wonder you saw beauty when I could only see the filth... no wonder you gave your all for this garden... no wonder you care for it more than I do... you are its original designer, so of course, you see its value! This is why you paid such a high price to buy it back... because you created it! It belongs to you!"

Now I understood why the Gardener never made me feel ashamed about the vast amounts of rubbish that once sprawled across its landscape. In fact, that's why he immediately removed it - he knew it didn't belong there. He understood the glory of its destiny and envisioned the garden exactly as he designed it to be from the beginning.

I stood in silent wonder, amazed at my newly-acquired revelation. Meanwhile, the Gardener continued working, although I knew full well he was aware of my contemplations.

After a while, he looked over at me and asked, "A penny for your thoughts?"

Without hesitation, I took off my shoes and plopped down in the soft grass.

"This grass feels amazing... would you join me for a minute?"

"That sounds good... then we'll need to get back to work!"

"So where is your penny and I'll tell you my thoughts," I smiled as I playfully elbowed the Gardener. "Seriously... I'm beginning to understand why everything you do makes me feel so complete and whole inside! This gives me an even greater reason to celebrate this day! To think at one time, I didn't even know you... and thought this land would never amount to anything but a pile of dirt!"

"That's the problem," the Gardener responded, furrowing his brow. "Everyone has a plot of land that's meant to be a garden. Most gardens end up trashed because people don't understand their true destinies. Others often sell all they have to buy the land, but use it to build high-rise buildings, theme parks, stores, or warehouses. They hope these things will fulfill them in one way or another. Some people even expand their houses onto the whole plot leaving only enough room for a tiny token garden that lacks any real glory or beauty. They think all these things will satisfy them and somehow enable them to succeed and be happy. Yes... everyone is trying to find value and meaning in life through their little plot of earth. Their feeble plans are nothing more than an all-consuming false identity that cannot bear fruit. And they do not understand that the land cannot thrive until it is created into a garden by its Gardener."

"And you *alone* know how to cultivate their plots into what you designed them to be," I interjected.

"You're right, only here will they find the life they are craving... all other attempts will fall short of true beauty and purpose!"

"Well... we need to tell them!"

"Yes... if they cannot see more, they will never expect more!"

"I experienced this first-hand! What a miserable existence I lived before I met you. I can't imagine ever going back. Like my garden, I'm a new creation flourishing with life!"

Just then, a dove flew overhead leading a parade of creatures into the garden. Behind him were bees, butterflies, bunnies, hedgehogs, frogs, ladybugs, caterpillars, and squirrels, all seeking shelter.

"Where are they coming from?" I giggled.

The Gardener stood with his arms crossed and grinned from ear to ear, apparently expecting their arrival.

"Oh, I invited them... they're our new residents! This is their new home where they can safely lay their young."

What a wonderful place to raise a family! Neither fear nor death loitered in the garden before the Gardener quickly replaced it with his pure love. Yes, he fathered the whole garden with his life, and in turn it flourished under his care.

"Look how many animals are flocking in! Will we need more space for them? Do you ever wish I had a bigger garden?"

"It's perfect... little is much when I AM in it. There is plenty of room for all!" he replied with a beaming smile. "Now, Birdy, it's time to get back to work... will you help me look for any loose bricks that might need repointing?"

"Sure, but I don't know what 'repointing' means."

"It means to secure those loose bricks with cement. You may have to use your eagle eyes because some cracks are hidden under the hedges."

I followed him through the bushes scouring the wall when my bare foot suddenly hit what felt like a rock.

"Ouch! I just stubbed my big toe on something really hard!" I yelped.

"Are you okay?" the Gardener asked as he knelt down to carefully examine my injury. "I'm so sorry... that can be very painful."

"I think I'm okay... but you know me... I don't like pain. I suppose no one does for that matter."

"What did you hit it on?"

"I can't see anything but ferns."

I bent down and pushed the shrubbery to the side. To my

~ *"Little is much when I AM in it."* ~

surprise, I discovered an old, moss-covered board. Together we lifted it off and found a circle of bricks on the ground.

"What is it?"

"It looks like a well!"

"Are you sure... I didn't know it existed... right here in my garden?"

"Great work finding it!" the Gardener responded, trying to cheer me up. "There are many more unseen things in your garden that await your discovery. Shall we have a look inside?"

"It's so dark I can't tell how deep it is," I said, peering into the opening.

Not wasting a moment, he picked up a small stone and threw it down the old well. With his hand to his ear, he listened for it to hit bottom.

"It's a good deep well!" he smiled.

"Hmm... I didn't hear a splash..." I countered in defeat, still feeling cross from the pain in my toe. "It looks like it's been dried up for years!"

"Dried up?" he chuckled with his hand on his hips as if I challenged his very life. "Do you want to help me fix it up?"

"Why should we? It's just an empty old hole in the ground, plus we have no way to fix it."

"Is that what you think?" the Gardener confidently grinned.

As hard as I tried, I couldn't see what he saw. Instead, my mind flooded with every excuse as to why we couldn't fix the well.

"We just need to cover it up again and forget the whole thing. I don't think it's worth the trouble!"

But the Gardener would not allow me to talk about what I couldn't see, couldn't do, didn't have, or lacked in any way. He always said, 'You will only see a lack in this garden when you are not seeing my ability and supply.'

"Birdy, celebrate it!"

"Celebrate what?"

He looked up from the old well into the well of my thoughts and gently but firmly answered, "*Life!* Celebrate what I can do and want to do and will do, rather than mourn what hasn't been done or what you're unable to do. That is what thankfulness is! It's an awareness and celebration of what's already been given to you. Thankfulness fills every heart with expectation... it is from this place you will find a spring that never runs dry!"

The Gardener envisioned a well of life while I stood paralyzed by the empty hole I accidentally stumbled upon. No, I didn't feel happy about my toe, nor was I thankful for the dried-up well. Frankly, all of it left me in a bad mood. But he refused to allow me to live in the barrenness of my half-empty cup and quickly put my hands to work. Together we began to restore the old well one brick at a time. First, we rebuilt the base. Next, he sent me on a mission to find a sturdy rope and a new bucket. Meanwhile, he added posts on each side of the well and tiled its roof. Upon returning, I handed him the bucket and rope.

"Thanks, these are perfect! I have high hopes for this well!"

It still didn't make any sense to me. Although I knew the garden belonged to the Gardener, and he planned to create it into the image of his own garden. So, at the end of the day, I suppose I just needed to trust him and be thankful.

After standing back to admire the finished product, he turned to me and asked, "Do you know the name of this well?"

"No... do you know its name?"

"It's called Rehoboth."

"Rehoboth?"

"Yes, Rehoboth! It means there's room enough for all to be loved in this garden! It lacks nothing! All are welcome to enter! Now go ahead and welcome this new well to your garden!"

"What do you mean, 'welcome it'?"

I didn't understand what he meant and felt a bit silly.

"Just say, 'Welcome to my garden, Rehoboth!' It's that easy!"

I looked at him and he gave me a wink and a nod, prompting me to go ahead.

"Okay... here goes..."

My eyes struggled to adjust to the endless darkness as I stared into the empty pit.

"Welcome to my garden, Rehoboth!" I reluctantly called out.

Rehoboth... Rehoboth... Rehoboth... echoed my words back to me.

Just as I turned away in disappointment, I heard the faint sound of my voice grow louder and louder. It sounded like tiny angelic voices trickling down in unison as they landed in a pool of water. When I looked back down into the well, I saw my reflection smiling up at me as the water began to rise.

"Where did the water come from? How in the world did it get in there?" I asked, baffled at the miracle before my eyes.

The Gardener simply smiled and answered, "Be assured, this well will never run dry again!"

"Never?"

"That's right... NEVER!"

How he got water into the bottom of that well, I couldn't tell you. But that's just what he did, and I was thankful! He viewed everything not for how it began, but for what he intended it to be. I guess that's why he didn't seem very pleased when I only allowed myself to see 'my less' above 'his more.'

In addition to the well, the Gardener also built other water features. Towards the front of the garden, he created a lily pond out of the mosquito-filled swamp I inherited. Now it bubbles with fresh water, lush lily pads, and a stunning array of fish. But his most majestic creation, is the beautiful fountain that stands in the center of the garden.

The Gardener unearthed its source one hot summer afternoon. Like a man on a mission, he set out to remove a cluster of big rocks in the center of my garden. As he dismantled the last boulder, the fresh spring erupted right out of the ground. After he uncovered it, he didn't stop working until its waters flowed freely. I remember hearing him laugh with excitement as it began to gush its way out of the earth's prison. He immediately knelt down to wash his hands in the fresh water, and then cupped his hands and took a drink.

"How does it taste... is it clean?" I asked, wanting to try some myself.

"Oh, it's absolutely pure and delicious... come join me!" he invited as he playfully splattered me with the cool water. "It's a good fountainhead... it will never run dry! Every garden has a spring waiting to well up... and I'm happy to announce yours has rich living water!"

"I've never tasted water this good!"

The Gardener grinned from ear to ear in satisfaction as I drank from the spring.

"It's the best! Absolutely perfect!"

It wasn't long before he sculpted a glorious white marble fountain to house the never-ending supply of life-giving water. He made paths in every direction so it could be easily accessed. At the base, he chiseled the words, *Come and Drink of the Water of Life Freely*, inviting all to partake of its thirst-quenching flow. The fount's mist gave refreshment to the nearby plants and cooled visitors on sweltering summer days. Its surging cascades melded into a symphony of beautiful music that soothed the soul. Of course, the fountain's exquisite design looked like it came directly from heaven. Well, it was the Gardener's masterpiece! Need I say more?

"You seem awfully quiet, like you're deep in thought," the Gardener said, bringing me back to the moment. "Would you like to join me for afternoon tea made from our *new* well water and tell me what's on your mind?"

He gave me one of his irresistible grins.

"Thanks, I'd love to!"

I followed him over to the little wooden table he built and sat down across from him.

"How are you doing?" he asked as he poured me a cup of hot tea.

"Well, honestly, this morning, I began the day celebrating all you have done... but for some reason, after I stubbed my toe, I lost the plot."

Wiggling my toe, I could still feel a dull ache.

"What really bothers me... is why I let the silly pain in my toe speak louder than everything you have already done?"

~ *"Be assured, this well*
will never run dry again!" ~

The Gardener didn't answer. Instead, he handed me milk for my tea. As I reached over to get the sugar, a bee landed on my spoon. Startled, I dropped it on the table and bolted from my seat.

"Oh no, now he's in the sugar bowl! I don't like bees!" I screeched.

"No need to fear! This little insect is our garden's best friend. Sometimes we miss the biggest blessings because we view them as our greatest threats!"

"I suppose you are right... but I've never liked bees!" I frowned, fighting the urge to run in the opposite direction.

After the bee tasted the sugar, it promptly flew towards the garden wall and settled on an old broken-down timber box under the honeysuckle vine.

"Come on back and have a seat, Birdy," the Gardener bid with a lighthearted chuckle.

"I'm not using the sugar after a bee's been in it!"

"Well, let's see if we can find something else to sweeten your tea with!"

The Gardener stood up and walked over to the worn-out crate.

"We need to get rid of that dilapidated thing! How did we miss it?"

Without responding, he pulled his penknife out of his pocket and carefully pushed the cracked boards off to one side.

"What are you doing?"

"Making your tea sweet!"

All at once, a stream of bees buzzed out the opening, ready for a mission.

"Oh no... what have you done?"

"Fear not, my dear! These bees aren't threatened... rest assured they won't sting us. They are on their way to find more nectar."

~ "Sometimes we miss the biggest blessings because we view them as our greatest threats!" ~

78

He reached in with his knife and carefully lifted out a scoop of honey from the honeycomb and brought it back to the table.

"Here you are! It doesn't come any sweeter than this!"

The Gardener grinned and licked off the little bit of honey that trickled onto his fingers.

"Wow! I never expected to find a beehive hidden right here in my garden. What a surprise!"

I scooped the honey off the Gardener's knife and stirred it into my tea.

"Mmm... this is really delicious! It's made ordinary tea into a gourmet beverage... thank you!"

"You're welcome!"

"Okay... now... where were we before the bee interrupted our conversation? Oh yeah, now I remember! I was disappointed with my bad attitude this afternoon. I guess what I'm wondering is... how do I guard my heart against these miserable mindsets?"

I took a sip of my tea and awaited the Gardener's response.

"That's a good question, Birdy... do you know what your part is?"

"What is my part?" I asked, setting my teacup down to give him my full attention.

"Expect from me, my life, my ability, my vision, my purposes, my directives, my love... expect from me all the time... and live from there! When I give you my word, know... with me... a promise is a promise."

He spoke passionately, as if he were giving me one of his most important keys to life.

"Expect good from you... even when I stub my toe or only see a dry, empty well?"

"Yes, expect even when a bee lands in your sugar bowl... or when you can't see the finished product of my creation! Every single moment of every single day... EXPECT! Remember when this plot was nothing more to you than a wasteland? Look what I did with it! Today, you lost sight of my ability... that's why you ended up with a bad attitude."

"Yeah... I know! When I forget all you have already done, I'm quick to despair over the different needs I see around me. You turned this old, useless dirt into a heavenly sanctuary of life. Now it continuously overflows with satisfying water so all can come and drink freely. You revived it with life! Yes, I need to learn to EXPECT more from you, don't I... but how do I remember in those difficult times?"

"Thankfulness enables you to see what I have already done... what I AM doing... and what I ultimately will do. This helps build your expectation. Yesterday's thankfulness births today's expectancy."

"You are right! Oh, to be able to see through your eyes. What a wonderful place where no fear can dwell. In reality, every adverse situation, is a place of thanksgiving - because I know you are at work. I want to learn to see life this way."

The Gardener looked at me with his kind eyes and gave me a big, happy smile.

"Your garden's re-creation is my recreation. It's what I delight in. Re-creating it into the likeness of my own garden..."

"...which is a beautiful sanctuary bubbling with all-sufficient life!" I smiled, finishing his sentence.

What more could I EXPECT?

I could celebrate!

~ *"Expect from me, my life, my ability,*
my vision, my purposes, my directives, my love...
expect from me all the time...
and live from there!" ~

CHAPTER 7

The Inspector

Filled with anticipation, I arrived at the garden before sunrise. A distinct quietness resonated in the air, filling me with a divine sense of holy awe.

"Good morning! What a delight to see your lovely face so early!" the Gardener welcomed with his customary cheerfulness. "Come on in and let me lock the gate."

"Why do you need to lock it?" I asked a bit puzzled.

"There are times we need to be extra careful," he replied with a concerned look. "Would you like to join me on the swing?"

"Yes, I'd love to!"

I followed him over to our secret place and nestled myself close to him. Today I noticed the Gardener spoke with a serious but tender tone - each word intentionally communicated to prepare me with his perspective and truth for the day.

"Life is filled with tests, Birdy... but remember, I know the answer to every problem concerning this garden. If you ask for my help... I promise to always be there!"

Distracted by a ladybug that landed on the back of my hand, I gave the Gardener a half-hearted nod.

"Well, we have *no* problems today! Everything seems perfectly in order!" I smiled, relishing his peaceful presence.

That is, until the glorious morning came to a screeching halt. Out of nowhere, a harsh voice boomed from the front gate.

"Open up right now! I'm on official business!" the voice demanded.

"Who is this guy... I wonder what he wants?"

Before the Gardener could respond, I grabbed his key and abruptly left him to open the gate. To my surprise, I encountered a tall, lanky stranger with dark beady eyes and thin pursed lips peering over the wall. Behind him stood his three apprentices, all wearing dark sunglasses.

"Why are they here?" I said under my breath.

The leader wore a pinstripe suit with a yellow hard hat that covered his black hair. A silver pen stuck out behind his pointy ear and on his lapel sat a gold authoritative-looking badge stamped Inspector. He looked like he belonged on a construction site.

"Hun, I've come to inspect your garden! We've gotten such bad reports about all its problems... and Chicky, it's your lucky day... we're here to help sort them all out!" he grimaced, looking down his nose at me.

"Y... yes, Sir!"

I unlocked the gate and stepped back, not sure what to expect next. This Inspector guy barged right past me toting an official-looking clipboard with a checklist a mile long.

"Let's go, gang," he ordered to his peevish-looking assistants.

Something didn't seem right! I never knew that gardens needed inspection! At first, he acted like an angel of light sent to illuminate me with his seemingly excellent knowledge. His words oozed like honey as his interrogation began. He tried hard to keep his composure, but his malicious anger quickly seeped into condemning words. His overbearing manner made me feel very uneasy. And why all the harsh, intimidating language?

"Who gave you planning permission to restore this garden? Tell me why you haven't secured an aqua license for this fish pool? Oh no no no, look at this dangerous well... anyone could fall into it! And who made this despicable fountain of so-called living water... it's all unacceptable!" he sneered as he scribbled something on his clipboard.

He then marched over to the marble fountain and slapped a 'CONDEMNED' sticker on it.

"You gotta get rid of this immediately!" he growled. His eyes blazed with fury as his cross-examination pressed on, "Are the fish properly tended? What kind of wood did you use to build the benches... they don't look sturdy to me! What kinds of plants do you have in this place? Who gave you permission to plant them? Why haven't you sprayed the trees and fruit with insecticide? And who said you could plant organically? Don't you know there are aphids, grubs, and other dangerous insects? What kind of animals live in the garden? Why haven't you reported them to animal control? Do you have all my mandatory vaccinations? What forms do you use to register people who visit this so-called garden of yours? What do you communicate to them? Do you have insurance for every kind of hazard that might ever occur?"

Question after question bellowed out of this bony man with a gruff voice. The list seemed endless. After a while, I felt very intimidated and completely worn down. Every time I tried to answer him, he interrupted me with a smirk of displeasure, which made me grovel even more in humiliation. Before I knew it, I found myself apologizing over and over again - and for what, I didn't have a clue.

And if that wasn't enough, he and his mob surrounded me like vultures after a fresh kill. They spat insult after insult in my face hoping to strip me of every last bit of dignity and honor. Hunched over in defeat, I turned to walk away when the Inspector grabbed me by the arm.

"Where do you think you're going? We ain't finished yet!" he hissed.

Why couldn't he at least smile or speak kindly? Instead, he continued his ongoing probe. Would it ever end? An awful fear gripped my heart when I realized his critical list had only just begun. In utter distrust, I silently watched as he scrutinized every inch of the garden.

"I wonder what he'll disapprove of next," I anxiously mumbled.

"Speak up, girl! Are you afraid to talk or what? You should be thankful I'm here! Oh, you're so lucky I've come to show you all your problems."

His condescending words cut me up into tiny pieces.

"I'm doing you such a favor not charging you full price for this inspection. However, you're gonna have to pay all the fines you've incurred. It's your own fault! You need to be more open-minded and rethink your values and ideals if you ever want to succeed," he howled.

Once again, we found ourselves at the fountain. The Inspector appeared particularly bothered by it.

"By the way, do people drink from this fountain? Have you tested it for parasites? It's probably contaminated. It's totally unfit for human consumption. Also, this sign at the bottom, *Water of Life*, is false advertising! Rumor is, you will never thirst again when you drink from it. What a joke! Yes, the whole thing's gotta come out soon as possible," he roared, looking pleased with himself.

Paralyzed with fear, I felt my face turn red and hot. What have I done? I trusted the Gardener, but maybe I shouldn't have. The water seemed pure to me. I drank from it every day and always felt refreshed and renewed. These were the hard facts I tried to remind myself of amidst all the confusion. The Inspector spoke with a tone of authority, but completely twisted the truth and left out essential information. His unwarranted behavior made me angry.

"Sir, these accusations are false!"

"Shut up child, before I double your fines! Show me just one permit you got for this garden... you can't... because you don't got any!" The Inspector let out a wicked laugh and continued to grill me, "This insolence will cost you... you'll have to work for me... the rest of your life!"

I wished I hadn't opened my mouth. What a huge hole I'd dug for myself! How could I have failed so miserably? I thought about all the permits I should've secured but didn't realize were needed. What a mess I'd gotten myself into.

"I guess I just need to shut down the whole garden," I groaned in defeat.

With his hands on his hips and a snarl on his face, the Inspector triumphantly announced, "Now you're talking, young lady! You're finally seeing the light... this garden's always gonna be a disgusting waste place! What a shame! It's all gotta go! This is your *new* normal... get used to it!" Then turning to his gang, he cackled, "Let's get out of here, boys, we've done our job. I'm getting rid of this whole pathetic place!"

Meanwhile, they danced around me and scornfully chanted, "Yeah! It ain't no good! You messed up bad! There ain't no hope! Run, and don't look back!"

I wanted to cower and hide, but I couldn't escape. Fear gripped my stomach and knotted it into a ball. Overwhelmed and trapped, I buried my face in my hands and sobbed. In a moment of realization, I remembered the Gardener had warned me about the dreaded Inspector and his crew. Why did I allow them to come into my garden? Why did I try to handle this whole situation on my own? The garden belonged to the Gardener. He certainly would know what to do!

"Master Ga..." I squeaked out in a feeble whimper.

Instantly, my dear Gardener stood by my side. With a stern, authoritative look, he walked over to the Inspector and tore off his badge.

"It's fake!" he said as he flipped it over, exposing its complete illegitimacy. "He's a phony and a counterfeit! He hates this garden's transformation and came to destroy it today!"

The Inspector, or whatever he was, immediately backed away in fear towards the gate with his cronies trembling behind him.

The Gardener then turned to me and said, "This one has no legal right to be here. This garden is private property that I bought and paid for years ago. I've already secured all its licenses and permits in perfect accordance with the law. You owe him nothing! This snake is an imposter and a liar who is only here to steal, kill, and to destroy!"

With absolute authority, the Gardener turned and shut the gate in the face of the self-proclaimed Inspector. The serpent rapidly slithered away from the garden - no words were needed. No one could question who was in charge now.

Still, I shook from the whole dramatic ordeal and my heart pounded out of control. My mind scrambled to sort out the lies and repossess the truth in light of all the Gardener declared. Suddenly my thoughts gravitated to the brown leather folder. It proved with certainty this garden belonged to him. He finished the legal battle required to take ownership of it long ago. So why did I believe the mendacious and accusatory Inspector for even one second? The sting of his dark trickeries left me raw inside. Why did I allow his defiling words to touch me?

As I tried to rein in my desperate thoughts, the Gardener took my hand and began to calm my fears.

"You know, I have already accomplished everything needed for you and your garden. No one has the right to take from you what they did not give to you in the first place. You must always trust my work because it's all you will ever need!" he reassured with a soft but confident voice.

The Gardener then showed me his scarred hands. They reminded me that I never needed to doubt his word again.

"I can see so plainly... you already paid for it all," I sighed in relief. "How did that beast even get into my garden?"

"Remember... you took the key and left me on the swing to go unlock the gate."

He spoke gently, without a hint of reproach in his voice.

~ "No one has the right to take from you what they did not give to you in the first place." ~

"What was I thinking? I gave you the key... why would I take it from you? Why didn't I let you decide whether to open the gate or not? Why did I leave you this morning?"

I reached into my pocket and immediately returned the key to him. He didn't see the need to answer any of my questions. Instead, he began to explain the imposter's identity and what kind of evil plans he devised to destroy my garden and me.

"He's an old enemy of mine who wants your plot of land for his own evil agenda. He's looked for ways to deceive you from the beginning. I've seen him pace up and down outside the walls looking for a chance to come in and destroy your garden. His mission is to try to stop me from creating each garden into its purposed destiny... which is to bear my image... and to keep everyone from having a garden. He executed his plan today but failed. You must be aware the angry loser will come again if he sees an opportunity. Next time, he won't mislead you because you have my truth as your guard. Since he cannot destroy the work in this garden, he will try to discount it in every way possible. You must walk in my authority alone and silence the lying trespasser. He wants people to think their lives will never amount to anything more than a forsaken plot of dirt. Those who believe his lie give him the power he needs to bring about their demise," the Gardener resolutely declared.

"Well, he sure did a good job of making me feel like dirt today!" I shuddered as a nasty chill ran down my spine.

"Birdy, my dear child... do not acquiesce to his doom-spun rhetoric! You are *more* than dirt! I deliberately created your garden to be a receiver and bearer of the life I plant into it!"

The Gardener paused to console my brokenness with a smile of hope.

"The truth is... no one is dirt to me! I need to remove this lie from every person so they can see they are more than dirt. Each plot's identity and destiny is to be a flourishing garden filled with my life... this is my eternal narrative for you!"

With a twinkle of delight in his eye, he reached down and picked up a handful of soil. After examining it for a moment, he kissed it and let it sift through his fingers back to earth.

"Once you understand and believe this garden is created by me, bought by me, and now restored by me, you'll see no one else has the right to tell you differently. That slithering viper will never be able to lie to you... ever again. The Inspector is the father of lies. When he speaks, you can know with certainty the opposite of what he says is true. Then his lies will drop to the dirt. If you believe his lies, you will be bound up in confusion. But when you know and live in my truth, you will be set free. Now be at rest! Know to whom you belong and live in the truth of who you genuinely are. Be strong and courageous! Don't ever be afraid of him! You must stand in my full authority! Remember, you never have authority over what you fear. Whatever you let author your reality is what you will fear. Remain with me, and you need never worry!"

He drew me to his side and gave me a great big hug, and boy, did I need it! The instant he wrapped his strong arms around me, I felt every last fear disappear, and my whole body began to relax. He truly was my safe place. The evil thoughts and feelings planted by the Inspector immediately dissipated. In its place, the Gardener sowed his treasured peace.

"This peace cost you everything... didn't it?"

"Yes... now it belongs to you! You may share it with everyone... but you must not give it away to anyone!" he instructed.

I was free! His truth had set me free, and no one had the right to take it from me again.

"I don't ever want to be ignorant of the enemy's devices! I forgot who you created me to be... and who my garden belongs to... didn't I?"

"Birdy, you're a reflection of my goodness... I purchased every bit of this garden... and no one can take that from you!" he affirmed with a confident smile.

"I didn't do very well on my test today, did I?"

"Well... you *did* call out to me!"

"And *you* helped me pass the test... just like you promised. I'm sure glad you keep your promises! Thank you for rescuing me... and thank you for protecting me and providing everything I need for this garden to thrive! I can't imagine living under the Inspector's tyranny! Thank you, my one and only true Gardener! Thank you! Thank you!"

"That's what a *true* Gardener does! Now let's not let our enemy steal another second of our time. He's a defeated foe! And we have a whole day ahead of us filled with lots of guests to love."

"I can't think of anything else I would rather do... to love freely... with no one breathing down my neck!"

"Never be afraid to love, my dear... there is no law against loving... and there is no fear in love... and perfect love casts out all fear!"

"Well... if perfect love casts out all fear... I think this garden needs a big dose of love after this morning's events! The fake Inspector wanted to stop me from loving people... but he didn't succeed."

The Gardener put his arm around me as we walked over to the gate. By now, a long line of visitors gathered waiting to come in. After giving me the 'go ahead and open the gate' nod, we began to love all who entered.

I knew it would be a wonderful day... because... love never fails.

~ "Once you understand and believe
this garden is created by me,
bought by me, and now restored by me,
you'll see no one else has the
right to tell you differently." ~

89

CHAPTER 8

Pruning

"Oh no! I slept right through my alarm!" I groaned as I silenced the noisy clock.

I didn't feel up to par, which made me grumpy inside.

"Ugh... why am I so tired this morning? I want to stay in bed all day long... hmm..."

I pulled the sheet over my head hoping to escape life. All the while, I felt a gentle prodding inside calling me to arise and press on!

"I suppose I should probably get up and face the day... but on my terms!" I decided.

After a small breakfast, I shuffled out to the garden and quietly closed the gate behind me.

"I just want to be left alone... I need some 'ME' time. The Gardener will understand..." I said, trying to justify my rotten mood.

"Birdy... Birdy... good morning... I'm over here!" called the Gardener.

Still absorbed in my gloomy thoughts, I disregarded his call. I knew I should talk to him, but I didn't feel like it. Instead, I plopped down on an old stump near the gate and stared at my shadow on the ground. Apathetic and foggy-headed, my brain refused to engage in any clarity of thought. A collage of negativity swirled through my mind. The longer I sat and brooded, the wearier and more depressed I became.

"Good morning!" greeted a voice behind me.

Curious and a bit annoyed at the interruption, I turned my head towards the gate only to find a distinguished, well-dressed man peering over the top.

"Please forgive my intrusion! I am on my way to work, and I couldn't help but notice your garden as I walked by. At second glance, I found myself completely drawn to its beauty. I hope you don't mind that I stopped... I just wanted to get a better view. Again, forgive me..."

Where did this guy come from? I let out a loud sigh and looked him over once again. He gave me a pleasant grin and patiently awaited my response. He *seemed* like a nice man, and I knew inside that I should at least *try* to be polite to him.

In an effort to meet his professional courtesy with my own attempt at cordialness, I slid off the stump and walked over to the gate.

"Please don't apologize, sir. This garden is here for everyone to enjoy. It's a lovely garden if I do say so myself... you're more than welcome to come in and have a look if you'd like."

What did I just do? Why did I invite a perfect stranger into my garden? I didn't want to talk to anyone this morning!

"Oh well, grin and bear it," I muttered under my breath through a fake grin.

"I know these types of gardens don't just grow themselves. They take a lot of hard work and need a knowledgeable Gardener!" he noted, as if he too owned a garden. "Is it alright if I take you up on your offer and have a quick tour?"

"Sure, come on in... gate's already unlocked," I half-heartedly invited.

"Is all this your masterpiece?" he asked, letting himself in.

His eyes lit up as he perused the garden.

"Well, in a way it is," I chuckled with a slight toss of my head.

But as the words came out of my mouth, I felt uneasy and bothered. I knew very well the Gardener created the entire garden from start to finish.

"Would you like me to show you some of the rare flowers and fruit trees I planted?"

He eagerly nodded, and I set out to parade all my favorite spots before him. As we walked down the hidden paths, I called out each plant's name using the little bit of knowledge the Gardener had given me. Of course, I acted as if I spoke from my own expertise.

"Does the garden always look this perfect and pristine?"

"Oh yes... I tend it every day."

"Well, it's absolutely beautiful! Every part of it is just magnificent!"

I knew I genuinely impressed him, that much I could tell.

"And there's a lot more to show you... just follow me!" I pompously asserted as we rounded a bend in the path. "Oh no... what's all this!"

Our tour came to an abrupt stop when we encountered a big pile of freshly cut foliage blocking the way. Stacked on top were uprooted weeds, dirt and all. I examined the scene for a few seconds. Horrified by the mess, my face reddened with embarrassment. That ugly heap ruined my picture-perfect garden! I cringed inside, not sure what to say. What would my visitor think of me now that my garden looked less than flawless?

"Good morning, my dear Birdy!"

The Gardener poked his head around the corner and greeted me with a warm smile and bright, sparkling eyes.

"And who might this be with you?"

"Good morning, Sir! I guess you could call me a nosey neighbor just wanting to have a peek at this beautiful garden," the sightseer responded.

"How nice to meet you! I AM the Gardener, but I guess you can already tell by the roadblock I've created."

"Oh... so you're the Gardener here," he replied a bit puzzled.

The visitor stopped and scratched his head as if he needed to recalculate the whole morning.

"Well, it's nice to meet you too! May I ask... are you the mastermind behind this whole creation? It's a beautiful work of art! I love what you've created here!"

The stranger scanned the garden once again. He gave me a quick smile like he now saw more to the story than I initially communicated to him.

"Thank you! It is *indeed* my masterpiece!" the Gardener replied with a big honest grin.

"It's simply majestic in every way!" Then glancing down at his watch, he exclaimed, "Wow, I didn't realize the time! I need to be on my way, or I'll be late for work. Thank you for this pleasant expedition! I best be going now... what a pleasure to meet you both!"

"Oh, we're sorry that you have to leave so soon. Please do come again!" the Gardener bid as he shook our new friend's hand.

In the blink of an eye, our guest disappeared out of the garden. The Gardener and I stood alone with one another for what seemed like an eternity. His eyes twinkled as he smiled at me.

"Hello again, my dear Birdy... how are you doing today?"

I didn't want to answer him because I still felt a bit cross inside. Before I could inquire about what looked like wreckage in my garden, he handed me some clippers.

"Will you follow me? I have something I want to show you."

I reluctantly trailed behind him.

"Where are we going?"

"My dear... we are at our destination!"

The Gardener stopped and pointed at the white wooden arbor entwined with a beautiful grapevine in its lattice. Everyone who saw the vine loved it and commented about its massive grapes and how sweet they tasted.

"Notice the thriving leaves on this shoot between the branch and the vine?"

I nodded and leaned in to get a closer look.

"Well, these are called 'suckers.' They grow fast and furiously and look pretentiously promising - but in reality, they yield nothing but barren leaves. They are deceitful lies that steal the life from the grapevine - I call them 'weights.' They're life-takers that appear to be healthy leaves. But they weigh the branches down with foliage and demand life and energy from the vine. In the end, they yield no fruit and leave the vine drained of nourishment. These are what you saw on the path," he said as he clipped one off.

"Yeah... well, how about the rest of the plants in the pile?"

"Those, my dear, are weeds that have grown up among the other plants. Some are from the past, and some have come in with all the animals and people."

"Are they really weeds? They looked like healthy shrubs to me."

"Yes, Birdy. They appear to be lush and strong because they leached the nutrients from the other plants around them. The reality is, they are thieves. At the end of the day, they don't give life to the garden; they rob life from it. You see, the weeds want to live in this garden because the soil is so rich. But they miss the mark and do not belong here, so we must uproot them."

"Even if they are small... and look nice?"

"Remember, it's my job to keep this garden healthy, so it doesn't get sickly and unable to thrive... I only prune what I love! Pruning is not rejection and death... it's correction and enablement to flourish!" the Gardener replied as he wiped the sweat off his brow.

I knew he spoke the truth, but I didn't want to admit it. Filled with pride, I bit my lip, crossed my arms, and tapped my foot on the ground. Although inside, I hated how I felt. How did I get here?

~ "I only prune what I love!

Pruning is not rejection and death...

it's correction and enablement to flourish!" ~

Meanwhile, he lovingly explained his actions and calmly diffused my irritated feelings with his truth. As much as I fought to hold onto my stance, I secretly desired to be set free from the inner conflict of my self-imposed pontification.

But the Gardener's love would not let go. He glanced up from his work and looked deep into my eyes as if he could see my entire soul. In just a few seconds, my morning escapades flashed across my eyes, and I felt utterly exposed.

"I... I guess you see all the unhealthy and diseased parts of my garden... that I don't always see. You... you fully know me and my garden, don't... don't you?" I stammered, feeling humbled, convicted, and broken.

Why didn't I come to him first thing and simply tell him exactly how I felt? Why did I push him aside? After all, he truly loved me. His very presence is what infused me with strength - it's what I needed most. That decision led to the rest of my poor choices, each one as unproductive as those destructive weeds. Why would I try to take credit for his work? How could I do this to him? He alone created the whole garden from start to finish.

Disgusted with myself and full of guilt, I hung my head and looked at the ground in remorse.

"How did I get into such a mess in the first place? I just wanted a little bit of 'ME' time, and I ended up completely ruining my whole day!" I whimpered.

No longer able to hold back tears, I covered my face with my hands.

The Gardener put his hand on my shoulder and calmly spoke,

"Dear... the day has only just begun."

But it felt over for me! I kept my face hidden and didn't say a word.

"My dear... you don't have to hide your tears from me! Let me see your precious eyes," he said with a soft, disarming voice. "Did you hear me call your name when you entered the garden this morning?"

We stood in silence for a while until I finally looked up at him.

"Noo... I mean... yeees... I... I wasn't listening!" I confessed, shaking my head in shame. "I'm never going to change! I'm such a failure... such a BIG, BIG failure!"

"Just because you fail doesn't make you a failure... any more than mud on a flower petal makes the flower a mud puddle."

"Well, I still hate myself!"

But the Gardener would have none of that. He wiped the tears from my eyes and gently lifted my chin. As my eyes met his tender gaze, I knew he not only forgave me but also destined me to be so much more than I could see.

"I'm so sorry... so, so sorry!"

"Birdy... I don't want to see you go through life 'trying' to be special... when you already are. You must never forget you are fully known and fully loved. It's my love that validates you and covers you with honor. You cost me everything... that is your price tag. This whole garden is my gift to you which alone is enough... you cannot add to your value. You must live with confidence in what I've already done for you. You must not give any lie the power to steal this truth from you. Otherwise, it will rob you of your very life."

As he replaced the prideful lies with his humble truth, all my feelings of confusion and lack of self-worth transformed into grateful appreciation.

~ *"You must live with confidence in what I've already done for you."* ~

"So why did I think I needed to impress anyone to begin with?"

"You must grow to understand who you are... and begin to live from this place. Remember, I could see a garden back when everyone else only saw an empty dirt field... and I loved it then as much as I do now. I already gave all to validate your garden with my love. You need no other source of worth! As you comprehend my love, you'll understand who I created you to be."

The Gardener's words infused my soul with his life, like warm sunlight on a winter day.

"Your performance never gave you true worth and never will. Real fruit can only be born when you live from the validation of *my* love... if you try to manufacture fruit apart from the tree, it will always be inedible plastic fruit with no real life."

"Are you saying there is no need for me to prove myself to anyone ever again... and... the only way I'm going to be able to live in this place... is to grasp your unconditional love for me? I want this truth to be fully rooted in my heart... so that none of those deceptive 'suckers' or weeds will ever get the chance to steal what you've already given me... ever again! Why would I want to manufacture my own artificial fruit when you've given me the real thing? I... I desperately need your love to be my greater reality. Please... will you help me understand this? What do I need to do?"

"There is nothing you need to do but simply accept what I've already given to you. Seek me first, spend time with me, and get to know me more intimately. It is in this place you will grow to know my love. Take all I have done personally... so you don't see yourself apart from my love. Every time you choose by faith to trust my love, your revelation will deepen and infuse you with strength. Remember, this is who you are and how you will thrive with life."

I breathed a sigh of relief as the dark, empty shadows of my counterfeit thoughts vanished and radiant joy burst through my soul.

What would I do without my Gardener's continual wisdom and loving care? What would I do without his constant watchful eye? Who else knew every intricate detail, and plant name in this garden? He never uprooted one innocent plant by mistake nor accidentally nipped a single leaf when he extracted what didn't belong. Who else could I trust to be more knowledgeable and more caring than he? He ever-tended and protected my garden, and no one loved it as he did. Yes, he fully knew and fully loved my garden, just as he did me.

Suddenly the Gardener put one finger to his lips as if to say, 'Be still!' With his other hand, he pointed to the rosebush near the swing.

What did he see?

At second glance, I saw a beautiful doe with her speckled fawn. We silently watched as they licked the inside of the roses. Like a bear with a honey jar, they eagerly tasted every last drop. The mother then noticed us out of the corner of her eye and gave her little one a quick 'We must go!' nod. In a flash, they disappeared.

"What were they doing?" I whispered, still in awe.

"They came to drink the dew that collected in the roses last night. The sweet water remained locked at the base of each petal awaiting their thirsty tongues," he explained.

"That's amazing! They could have drunk water from the pond, but they chose to drink from the roses... why?"

"It is their prized cup they drink from... filled with goodness... and as you can see, the deer came to the garden to find it."

The Gardener paused and put his hand on his chin, deep in thought.

"Did you know, at night, when the flowers and leaves are quiet, their pores open to receive the refreshing dew? Absolute stillness is required to prepare the plant before the water can collect on its petals and leaves. Dew will never gather while there is heat or wind."

I listened very carefully as he continued to expound.

"You, my dear, can only find your morning dew when you quietly wait to meet with me. In this place of silence you will find yourself saturated with my presence. Only then can you go forward in your day invigorated, instead of empty and drained. Just as the deer panted for the water in the roses and found satisfaction... you also will find refreshment and be renewed with the morning dew when you meet with me. My quietness and rest always strengthen you with life."

"Now I understand! While I sat on my little stump tired and flustered this morning... trying to get some 'ME' time... you awaited me with your dew of life!"

"Yes, I will always await you here!" he promised, giving me a warm smile. "Our connection is where you will find your sufficiency..."

"... and my true rest. That's what I needed this morning... but didn't realize it! No one but you can fill my void... or give me the life I need to go forward. I must intentionally receive my morning dew... early... before the heat of the day or the winds set in... this will change everything!" I said, taking a moment to reassess the whole morning.

The Gardener put his arm around me and began to softly hum an old tune.

He paused for a moment and assured, "The love we share when we tarry in this place... together... will become the abundant joy you need to live your life."

"Nothing compares to your perfect love... it's the prized cup I drink from! It has given me true honor and value... I don't need to go anywhere else... you're my dew of life!" I whispered as I laid my head on his chest.

"Yes, my dear Birdy... my love is enough... always enough!"

My soul quieted into complete peace.

~ *"In this place of silence you will find yourself saturated with my presence."* ~

CHAPTER 9

Emma

"Good morning, world!" I exclaimed through a happy yawn as I stretched my arms towards heaven. "What a glorious summer sunrise!"

As I headed out to meet the Gardener, I found new life bursting forth from every corner of the garden. The flowers smiled in full bloom, and the trees dripped in abundance with luscious fruit.

"Good morning, M'Lady!" the Gardener greeted as he opened the gate for me.

"And to you too!" I said with a curtsey. "Isn't this a beautiful day? Although every day is a wonderful day to you!"

"Indeed, it is!" he grinned as he surveyed the garden. "I have a surprise for you this morning! Just close your eyes, and I will lead you to it."

"What is it?"

"Don't peek! You will have to wait and see, my dear! You can trust me."

The Gardener held my hand and carefully led me to our destination.

"Okay... you can open your eyes now!"

"Wow! What a pleasant surprise!"

There under the willow tree, stood a little white wooden table with a vase of newly-cut daisies. At each place setting sat an indigo blue bowl filled with fresh fruit salad topped with a dollop of yogurt.

"Welcome to my Garden Café! Won't you have a seat at my table? Now... how about a glass of our homegrown fresh-squeezed orange juice, or would you prefer a cup of my home-brewed coffee? Oh, and

I have homemade toast as well!" he chuckled.

"Your 'home' menu sounds wonderful... I think I'd like all of it, please!"

"Good choice!"

After serving me, the Gardener sat down at the table.

"This fruit is so delicious..."

"It is... the garden has produced an abundance of extra-large fruit this year... and it's extra-sweet! We can't possibly eat all of it by ourselves!"

"Maybe we could share our bounty with our guests!" I suggested through a mouthful of fruit salad.

"Yes, generous giving is the key to a prolific garden! If you sow sparingly you will reap sparingly... but if you sow bountifully... you will reap bountifully!"

I nodded in agreement, although I wasn't quite sure what he meant.

"Are you going to eat the rest of your fruit salad?" I asked as I emptied his bowl into mine.

"Help yourself, Birdy... I guess you already did!" he chuckled.

I gobbled down the last few bites and together we cleaned off the table.

"Thank you for the scrumptious homemade breakfast, created in your Garden Café! I feel like a queen!"

"Well, you are my princess!"

He affectionately smiled as we watched two white butterflies dance around us like children playing tag. The precious morning hours and surprise breakfast with the Gardener made me eager to welcome the rest of the day.

"What a perfect start to a perfect..."

But before I could say another word, a loud clanging noise at the gate interrupted us.

"Hellooooo... I'm here!" Verma abruptly announced in her larger-than-life voice.

Like a general leading the charge, she marched right into my garden with two empty grocery bags under her arm. A stream of visitors followed behind her and our day officially began.

Verma, a 'pre-garden' friend, visited regularly. Everyone described her as a bull in a china shop. Still as obnoxious as ever, her overbearing personality and piercing voice preceded her like a foghorn on a lighthouse. From the moment she stepped foot in the garden, she acted as if she owned it and barked orders to all who crossed her path. In *her* world, no one could ever do enough for her. Discontent with her own life, she felt entitled to everyone else's portion. Even when we showered her with an abundance of grace, she ignorantly hoarded it. Not to mention her need to criticize and scrutinize each person she met to make herself look better. Of course, she continually touted a double standard to omit herself from any accountability.

To be honest, my heart sank in dread whenever she entered the garden! Most days I simply tried to ignore her, but today, she especially annoyed me. Her thunderous commands resulted in one brutal assault after another. She relentlessly interrupted and dominated every conversation so she wouldn't have to listen to anyone's voice but her own. Truth is, I no longer knew what to do with her. Her problematic personality was nothing but a bundle of prickles that made me want to avoid her at all cost.

"Hello Verma... what are those bags for?"

"None of your business!"

"Oh... well, why don't we take a walk? I want to show you my new rosebushes," I offered, hoping it would distract her from further disrupting the peace.

"Why would I want to take a walk with you?" she huffed, plopping down on a bench next to a nice elderly man. "Who invited you here, mister? Scoot over!" she scowled.

Startled by her offensive tone, the sweet white-haired man looked up. Without saying a word, he kindly obeyed her rude command and moved down the bench.

But that didn't satisfy her and after a few moments she roared, "I don't want to sit here anymore... it's way too crowded... do you get what I mean, mister?"

And off she went to find her next victim. I gave the poor man a quick 'I'm so sorry!' look and proceeded to chase her around quenching the fires her thoughtless words kindled.

"What am I supposed to do with this woman? It's going to be a looong day... my grace has run out!" I said under my breath.

Suddenly the garden became strangely quiet, and I breathed a huge sigh of relief. Perhaps it would be a good day after all. Still, I had that nagging feeling you get when something's just not right - it was way too quiet. Honestly, I didn't trust her, not for one second!

Just then, the Gardener showed up in his usual, perfect timing. He looked into my eyes as if to say, 'Is everything okay?'

"Oh, I am so glad you are here! Guess what I've been doing all day?" I asked, fully aware he already knew everything that took place in the garden.

Before he could answer, Verma sauntered around the corner with her two big grocery bags crammed full to the brim. One bag bulged with the biggest, juiciest, most delicious fruit in my garden. She took all the choice apples, oranges, mangos, pears, cherries, plums, apricots, peaches, grapes, plus who knows what else. And of course, the other bag burst with an array of my most beautiful flowers. She literally picked every last bit of my garden's finest bounty.

"Are you serious?" I curtly mumbled, shaking my head in disbelief at the Gardener. "She didn't even ask me if she could pick anything! She simply helped herself to all of it! And she hasn't contributed one iota of work in my garden! Who does she think she is anyway? I'm so irritated! Furious is more like it!"

Just as I began to confront Verma, she flippantly bellowed, "I need to be on my way! I've got a busy day!"

Without even a thank you or one hint of appreciation, she marched out the gate with the richest crops ever grown in my garden. I couldn't believe my eyes! Patience ceased to be my virtue, and my blood boiled in contempt. To top it off, I felt irritated for getting upset in the first place. At my wit's end, I turned to the Gardener and unloaded every last complaint of my terrible, no-good day.

"Did you see all the fruit and flowers that Verma stole from me? I can't believe it... she is incorrigible! From now on she's not allowed in *my* garden... if we don't stop her, she'll destroy everything! She's ruined *my* perfectly good day!" I fumed.

The Gardener quietly listened while I played the victim card. Although after I finished, I felt more frustrated and depressed than when I began. I swallowed hard trying to dismantle the lump in my throat, but to no avail. On top of everything, an unexpected thunderstorm drenched us from head to toe.

"The closest shelter is the tool shed... let's go in there," the Gardener said.

He took me by the hand, and we made a dash for it. As he closed the door behind us, I found myself in a perfectly organized world of lawnmowers, tillers, rakes, and whatnot.

"I know we only have standing room in here, but at least it's dry!"

"Well, I'm completely soaked... and cold!" I moaned.

"You *are* shivering... here, take my jacket. The outside is wet, but the inside is still dry... it will keep you warm for now."

"What a miserable day it's been! It all started when Verma got here... I wish I knew what to do with her!" I whimpered.

Then with a calm voice, he asked, "Did you forget to love her today? You know Birdy, the life of the garden comes from the love that we give... that's the real fruit!"

"What? By the time she finished picking all my fruit I didn't have anything left to give her," I retorted. "Besides, I was way too busy trying to protect everything and everyone from her anti-social behavior! How could I find the time to love her? You know what she's like! Just hearing her voice puts me into survival mode. She's a threat to my garden... and I don't want her to ever come back!" I ranted, feeling fully justified.

"Birdy, do you know she has a garden that awaits her?"

"Well why doesn't *she* stay in her *own* garden and pick her *own* fruit?"

"She has no idea I purchased it for her... all she can see is an old dumpsite filled with flea-infested vermin. Your garden is her only source of refuge and peace. She comes here desperately needing to be loved... not just tolerated... all lasting fruit must be born out of love... otherwise, it will spoil," he gently explained.

"You know Verma isn't an easy person to love!"

"Truth is Birdy... her name isn't Verma... that's a nickname her enemies gave her years ago, and she knows no other name. Her real name is Emma, which means 'whole and complete.' You must treat her as Emma because that's who she is and what I desire to create her to be. I have a good plan for her, and I would like you to be a part of my plan... if you're willing."

I wasn't sure if I wanted to be a part of his plan. My thoughts still battled to see any truth above my own feelings.

"So... what about all the fruit and flowers she stole from my garden?"

"Remember the 'key' I gave you this morning at breakfast?"

"What key?"

"Generous giving is the key to a prolific garden... the more we share our fruit and flowers, the more abundantly they grow in return. Be assured... you cannot exhaust the love I've planted here. There will always be plenty for all who enter. Remember... I AM the protector of this garden... and the provider. Don't be afraid to give away the love I've given you... I have a never-ending supply! Freely you have received, so freely you can give! And you know... I love a cheerful giver... and forgiver!"

"Forgive her?" I balked, raising my eyebrows. "She hasn't even said she's sorry!"

"You can forgive her even if she never apologizes. Forgiveness is easy when you remember how much you've been forgiven of... then you will begin to see her the way I see her."

"What about when people do wrong things, don't we need to set them straight?" I blurted out, still looking for the last bit of justification for my actions.

The Gardener didn't answer my question, but instead glanced out the shed window.

~ *"Generous giving is the key to a prolific garden..."* ~

"It looks like the storm has passed... shall we go outside?"

As we opened the door, a little red fox ran right past us. I noticed a choice bundle of grapes in his jowl that somehow escaped Verma's hands. At first glance, the fox seemed friendly and almost tame. Yet as soon as he appeared, the bunnies scurried to their holes in fright. Even the squirrels dashed up the trees to safety. A sense of danger filled the air causing the birds to scuttle about and seek shelter. The Gardener immediately shooed the fox out of the garden while I stood stunned by the whole event.

"He didn't seem that dangerous at first, did he? He was quite a beautiful little fox, but very naughty for stealing my grapes. I suppose that's why they call him a sly creature?" I half-heartedly chuckled.

The Gardener rubbed his chin and appeared concerned, "This beautiful little fox came to steal and spoil the vines. He's like those selfish attitudes that appear harmless. Both foxes and attitudes pilfer the choice fruit meant for those who need it most. Like the fox, these attitudes look unassuming and innocent. But in the end, they rob our love and joy, leaving the garden without peace. These little foxes, or little attitudes, make us unable to see clearly or respond correctly. They will appear when you lose perspective of who you are and why this garden is here. My love must always be the loudest voice in this garden... and you've let Emma's voice speak louder than mine. This steals your ability to love her."

Deep down, I knew the Gardener was right, but I still wasn't ready to love her.

"Emma is not what the vermin have made her out to be. I want to make her garden look just like mine!"

The Gardener's compassionate words melted my heart. I could tell he loved her because he spoke about her with the same endearing tone of voice he used with me. At that moment, I realized he saw more than her hard, broken exterior. He knew who he designed her to be from the beginning.

"Yes... I suppose I let Verma... well, Emma's anti-social behavior speak louder than your love. How did I end up in this place?"

We stood silent for what seemed like an eternity while I reasoned with the truth. After a while, I looked up at the Gardener. He gave a gentle smile that slowly disarmed my inner battle.

"I guess I haven't been seeing very clearly, have I? In reality, Emma isn't the thief... it's my own attitude that's been the greatest threat. I suppose the fruit and flowers were safe all along. The real problem has been my own rotten perspective. *My* selfishness is like the 'seemingly' harmless little fox! When I tried to 'save' this garden... I lost its very reason for being... what was I thinking?"

I hung my head in remorse and stared at the ground.

"Birdy, remember... your failures do not define who you are any more than Emma's failures define who she is. My love alone is what qualifies each person to receive life here."

The tenderness in the Gardener's eyes reassured me once again that my actions lacked any power to alter his love for me.

"I am so, so sorry! I don't want 'wrong thinking little foxes' in my garden again... but I need your help!"

"You are growing, my dear! Follow me... trust *my* love... then you will not lack any fruit."

The Gardener smiled compassionately. He didn't condemn me, but rather restored me with his wholeness and grace.

"I have so much to learn! I suppose if I waited for everyone to be deserving of any kindness, I would have to disqualify myself first... I can't forget the dirt field where I began. Why should I feel threatened by Emma since you've already given *your* all to lavish me with a garden of life? Yes, every ounce of beauty in this garden is *your* handiwork. Freely I have received, so freely I must give! You've given me more than I could ever imagine or need!"

"That's what we talked about this morning... remember... generous giving is the key to a prolific garden."

"How did I forget your *key* so quickly?"

"Let me explain. When you focus your eye on the truth, you will be full of light. But if you focus your eye on the lies that others believe, you will be overshadowed with darkness. Remember... the love inside this garden is always greater than the darkness outside."

"You're right! I... I suppose it's not my job to fix her... I've been so busy shielding my garden from her darkness that I neglected to love her. I should have introduced her to the only one who could make her garden whole and full of light. I let the lies she believes about herself speak louder than your truth, haven't I? Honestly... shouldn't the truth of what I see speak louder than what she doesn't see? Will you please help me hear the voice of your love above all... so nothing can speak louder... even when it's screaming?"

~ "My love alone is what qualifies each person to receive life here." ~

Then as he so often did, he bent over and kissed the top of my head.

"I will... I love you Birdy! I've already given my all for you... all that is mine is yours... and I have a never-ending supply. Take, eat, drink freely of my love... and remember... true lasting fruit comes from giving others the love I've already given you. Now simply be what I have made you to be... that *is* who you are."

"What have you made me to be?"

I already knew the answer but wanted to hear him tell me again.

"You are a garden of love and life!"

He looked into my eyes as if to say, 'You are more than you see, don't sell yourself short.'

"I think I'm beginning to understand... I just need to relax and be the garden you made me to be! I'm not the Gardener of this garden... nor its owner... you are! And only as I surrender everything into your hands will I be able to see from your perspective and hear your voice above all others!"

"Yes... here you will thrive with abundant life and not just survive in life... then you can share your bounty freely!"

"Yeah... and be a cheerful giver instead of an old fruit miser!"

The Gardener chuckled and grinned like a proud parent.

By now, the evening sun radiated through the clouds painting the sky with vibrant reds, purples, oranges and yellows. After we bid farewell to our last guest, I let out a happy sigh. The busyness of the day quietly faded into stillness.

"Birdy, it's good so see you so at peace!" the Gardener said as he closed the gate.

"I am *now!* Your presence is my place of sweet rest... and I can't bear to live one moment outside of it... like I did earlier today!"

"You never have to... I AM yours for life... and nothing can change that!"

Peace ruled the garden once again. The path of love began to widen in my heart. Yes, the Gardener's love would be my life's proclamation and banner!

CHAPTER 10

Absolutes and Variables

"I can't believe the temperature this morning! It's already over a hundred degrees... and it's not even 8:30 a.m.," I groaned as I closed the gate behind me. "It's so hot! Why does the heat make me *feel* so lethargic... and *feel* so weary? I honestly *feel* miserable today... like I walked into the Sahara Desert!"

The scorching weather always made me *feel* exhausted and today was no exception. I wanted to give up and go home but I knew the Gardener awaited me.

"Hello... hello... HELLO... anybody here? Where are you... why aren't you answering?"

Frustrated, I parked myself in the nearest shade, hoping he'd find me, but to no avail. Before long, the sweat rolled down my face and my clothes stuck to my body. I looked around for something to fan myself with, and of course, found nothing.

'Where is the Gardener?' I wondered.

Meanwhile, the sun rose even higher until my last bit of shade disappeared. Even the grass showed displeasure with its browned, sun-scorched tips.

"Where *is* the Gardener, anyway?" I muttered aloud this time.

Everything seemed eerily quiet - a little too quiet, leaving me *feeling* very alone.

"Hmm... well, what should I do now? It *feels* like it's getting hotter by the second! Where is the Gardener? Maybe he doesn't like the high temperature either. I bet he decided not to meet me today. Or maybe he thought I wouldn't show up in this heatwave. Well, this is miserable... even a tiny cloud in the sky or a mild breeze would make my life more tolerable."

Instead, the fiery doldrums of despair held me captive.

"Where is the Gardener?"

I scanned the garden looking for him but didn't see or hear anything. If he is here, why would he ignore me? Is he angry with me? Have I upset him? My mind suddenly smoldered with flashbacks of my pre-garden life, which made me *feel* even more dejected. *Feeling* abandoned, I got up, traipsed over to the Gardener's cabin, and pounded on the door.

"Hello! Hello! It's me... Birdy!" I yelled, but no one answered. "Maybe he gave up on me? I would give up on me I guess. Perhaps the garden is too much work for him."

The blistering heat continued to sear my face. Now drenched in sweat, my spirit wilted in utter hopelessness. Something *felt* very wrong. What happened to all the animals? I didn't hear any birds singing or see any butterflies flutter about. The leaves on the trees even hung limp.

"Everyone must be home hiding from this horrendous furnace," I mumbled. "Why is it so quiet? I hate this eerie silence. Something is wrong! It *feels* like the calm before the storm!"

Suddenly a loud noise broke the stillness with a clapping sound that became louder by the minute.

"What's that noise? The Gardener will know what it is... where is he anyway?" I hollered, although I knew he wouldn't hear me over the ear-piercing sound. "What could make such a horrible ruckus? Where is it coming from? I wonder if this is what locusts sound like?"

The Gardener warned me about the damage they can do to gardens. I listened intently to the noisy little pests and quickly deduced it must be the dreadful clatter of locusts.

"Oh, no! If they're locusts, they'll eat every last bit of green in this garden... and destroy everything that I love!"

That old panicky *feeling* rose in my chest, and I wrung my hands in despair. The noise seemed to intensify by the second. It sounded like an army descending for battle. It wouldn't take long for them to devour the whole garden. I didn't know what to do! What could I do? I *felt* fully distraught by the Gardener's whereabouts and clueless how to handle the whole situation.

"Where are you when I need you most?" I yelled in distress. "You picked the wrong time to walk off the job! You're the Gardener... you should be here! You've met me every morning... but nope, not today! I give up... it's hopeless... completely hopeless!"

The sound of screaming locusts screeched through the garden. In just one morning, my whole life fell into shambles. Terrorized by the noise, I ran towards the greenhouse, hoping to shield myself from the blaring racket.

In desperation, I shouted for the Gardener, "WHERE ARE YOU? HELP! I NEED YOU NOW!"

Finally, I heard a faint yet familiar voice answer, "Here I AM... in the greenhouse!"

It was my Gardener! Had he been in the garden this whole time? Out of breath and choked up, I burst through the door.

"Where are you? I need you!"

"I'm right over here, my dear... just look up!"

I instantly found myself relieved and reassured by his presence but still struggled with *feelings* of frustration at his apparent absence.

"Where have you been? What have you been doing?" I interrogated, still *feeling* a bit abandoned.

The Gardener came out from behind the tomato plants holding a bucket in each hand.

"Good morning, Birdy!" he cheerfully greeted.

His eyes twinkled with the same delight that awaited me every morning.

"I've been right here in the garden watering all these droopy plants. I hoped you would come and find me and help give these little saplings a drink. They're pretty thirsty today!"

"Well, so am I," I snapped.

The Gardener wiped the sweat off his brow with the back of his sleeve. He gave me a concerned look and as usual, read my anxious thoughts.

"You know, I promised that I would never leave you... even when you can't see me. That is an absolute!"

He looked into my eyes as if to say, 'Fear not!' and gave me a gentle smile.

"Yes, but there's an emergency that needs your attention... and when I couldn't find you, I began to worry!"

"When you seek me... you will always find me. Now, what is this looming emergency in need of my attention?"

"Locusts! It sounds like there are thousands of them! Can't you hear them? They're all over the place! I'm afraid they'll devour the whole garden! I *feel* sick just thinking about it!"

"So... how many of these locusts have you seen?" the Gardener calmly asked.

"Well, I haven't actually seen any, but listen... can't you hear them?"

He set his buckets on the ground and asked me to follow him to the tool shed. He then bent down outside the door and picked up an old coffee can with tiny holes poked through its plastic lid.

"Here, look at these, Birdy."

He lifted off the lid. Inside, I counted nine grasshopper-like insects. Well, that's what they looked like to me anyway.

"Are these some of the locusts I heard?"

"To tell you the truth, these are not locusts, although they do look similar. They're called cicadas. They don't eat a whole lot of vegetation, but they sure make a big commotion. One of these larger species alone can produce a call above 120 decibels. So, you can imagine what nine of these noisy fellows sound like!"

He put the lid back on his insect coop and set it down on the ground.

"Are there any more of these cicadas in the garden?" I asked, still *feeling* anxious.

"These are the sole culprits of the loud clamor. I caught them this

~ *"When you seek me...*
you will always find me." ~

morning before you arrived," he offered with a triumphant grin.

"You mean to tell me... all that ear-piercing racket came from those insects... and I had nothing to fear all along?"

I now *felt* a bit silly about my unjustified *feelings* of panic.

"Yes, my dear, every bit of the uproar came from this noisy coffee can."

The Gardener gave me a slightly amused smile which made me *feel* better about overreacting. Then he motioned me to follow him again.

"Come with me... would you mind helping me water the remaining plants in the greenhouse? Here's a bucket."

"Where are you getting your water from?"

"The fountain, of course!"

"That's right! How did I completely forget about the fountain... when it's right in front of me? And I know it never runs dry! I could've come here and let its spray cool me down. Instead, I boiled in my own sweat and entertained every depressing thought."

"Here Birdy, sit down and have a nice cold drink, then follow me back to the greenhouse. I have a few seedlings left to water."

I gulped down the entire glass all at once. Instantly my body filled with life and vitality.

"That was deliciously refreshing - just what the doctor ordered! I could have been enjoying this water the whole time! Instead, I got caught up in a vacuum of worry and fear."

How did I become so anxious? Why did I let this heat melt me down into a pool of fear? Why did I think the Gardener might be mad at me? Why did I think he didn't want to be my Gardener? Why did I doubt his love and his constant presence? How did I end up in such a quandary when the answer existed right in front of me? Why didn't I press in and seek out the truth?

The Gardener sat on the edge of the fountain and put his arm around me.

"Come now... let's reason and talk about this together."

He spoke with tender compassion as if he knew my every contemplation.

"Tell me... what's going on inside you? Are you okay? You seem bothered about something!"

When I tried to answer, my emotions tangled up into a lump in my throat and I began to bawl. The Gardener quietly held my hand while I sobbed. He then gave me a big 'you're going to be okay' smile, which encouraged me to tell all.

"Well, I'm upset because it's been a hard day! And I worked myself up into a tizzy over basically nothing!"

"What do you mean, Birdy?" he asked, wiping away my remaining tears.

"I don't know... it just *feels* so hot today... which made me *feel* miserable by the time I got to the garden! And when I couldn't find you anywhere, I *felt* upset... I *felt* like you might be mad at me or that you left me... and when I thought I heard locusts, everything fell apart. I *felt* soooo afraid... I didn't know what to do... and when I found you... well... I *felt* like such a loser, especially when I realized they were not locusts! But what bothers me most is how freaked out I *felt* about a situation that I could've easily avoided! And... you know me... I can't escape *feeling* upset when things are out of order. How did I get to this place?"

"Did you notice how often you said, 'I *feel* or *felt*' in your response?"

"Yeah... I said it a lot!"

The Gardener sweetly grinned and rubbed his chin as if he were about to uncover something special.

"Let me help you, my dear! The problem arises when we base our emotions on what we see, smell, hear, taste, and *feel*... our senses. All these things are just circumstantial variables, which means they can change at any given moment. If you allow your variables to dictate your emotions first, you'll always become a product of what you are going through."

The Gardener paused and handed me a bucket.

"Here, can you fill it up for me? We need to give the last little tomato sprouts a drink, so they don't die of thirst!"

After we filled them to the brim, he glanced in my direction and gave a mischievous grin. Then with a twinkle in his eye, he emptied his whole bucket all over me.

"Oh, no!" I shrilled, fully soaked but wonderfully exhilarated by the cold, fresh water.

"Wasn't that delicious?"

"You'll find out soon... remember two can play!" I giggled.

Following suit, I rewarded the Gardener's gesture and drenched him from head to toe. He let out a big, deep belly laugh, which in turn made me giggle all the more. Now cooled off, we repeatedly poured bucket after bucket on each other.

"I think there's more water on the ground than in the fountain!" I said as I wrung the water from my hair.

"You're probably right, but the fountain will soon fill up again. How do you *feel* now?" he asked, wiping his face with his handkerchief.

"I *feel* amazing! I certainly don't *feel* like the same person who walked into the garden this morning."

"See how your *feelings* have changed... but it's just because your circumstances have changed! If you go through life reacting to every variable around you, your emotions will be all over the place. As a result, your ever-changing *feelings* will dictate your joy and peace."

"I know! I do that all the time... I'm up and down with every situation... like a rollercoaster inside... I don't like it though!" I confessed.

"Not to change the subject... we still haven't watered those little sprouts... and I know they're thirsty."

We headed back to the greenhouse and before I knew it, we'd given every last seedling a drink.

"Birdy, notice how happy they are already? And only a few moments ago they seemed almost dead!"

"You're right!"

"You see... the circumstantial variables made them appear as if they were dying, but the absolutes declared otherwise."

"Absolutes... what do you mean?"

"Absolutes are the things that will never change. Everything in this garden is founded on absolutes. For example, I AM the Gardener here. That's an absolute! I will never leave this garden... absolutely never! Another absolute is that I paid all I had to buy this garden so that I could restore it with my original design. This proves this garden is my greatest treasure... that is an absolute! One more absolute you must remember is, this garden will never lack anything because I AM its Gardener. I have the resources necessary to sustain it through every situation or trouble it will ever face. The most important absolute... is that I love you... and I love everything this garden represents... that will never change, no matter what. These are the absolutes that you must always factor in first... just as if you were tackling an algebra problem."

I must have appeared a bit puzzled, so he continued to elaborate.

"Stay with me just a little longer... you'll begin to understand. Remember when you used to solve algebra problems? Your teacher would always remind you to factor in the absolutes first, which are those numbers that will not change. After you factor in the absolutes, you factor in the variables... those are the things that can change. This is how we must factor everything in our lives. You have the constants, or absolutes, which are the things that never change and are like bedrock. Then you have variables, the things that are continually changing. These are the circumstances and situations you face every day. And with every circumstance you encounter, you must first factor in the absolutes of who I AM, what I have done, and what I AM doing. Then, factor in all the variables. These are all your little issues, problems, and troubles that must be submitted to the higher truths or absolutes. The outcome of the variables will be dependent on the absolutes. For example, today it *felt* sweltering, and you *felt* tired, you couldn't find me, and you heard strange noises that sounded like locusts. These are your variables, which could change in a single moment. The first thing you needed to remember... is that when you seek me, you will always find me waiting for you. I will never leave this garden! Once you factor in this absolute, the remaining circumstances, or variables, won't have the power to move you to unrest or fear. If you allow the variables to dictate your emotions first, you will always become a product of what you are going through."

I quietly nodded, beginning to understand.

"Know with certainty... you are a product of my absolute love and not a product of all the variables around you!" he whispered, giving me a tender smile.

"I think I get it! I just needed to do the math!"

I paused for a moment to recalibrate my mind and allow his truth to sink in before I continued.

"If I factor the true absolutes into my life first... and then add the variables... especially concerning the trials and problems I face... it would change everything, wouldn't it? I get it! It seems so simple when you explain it that way! How much easier life would be if I based all my *feelings* and emotions on your absolutes instead of the constant barrage of variables around me."

"So often these variables are nothing more than shadows! Every picture has shadows, but they are not the essence of the picture... nor do we focus on them. They only serve to enhance the picture's color and depth to its viewer. We do not say, 'what ugly shadows that forest has,' but rather, 'what beautiful trees are in this forest.' The shadows only serve as illusive non-realities that are ever-changing with the rising and setting sun. When our lives become filled with dark, troubling shadows that may seem larger than life, they only serve to bring depth to the greater picture. You must not focus on the needy shadows, or variables, when the absolutes of my love and my promises are painting a real-life picture of splendid glory."

"It's true! It's absolutely true!"

The Gardener gave me a wink and a nod. His pleased look let me know I comprehended his equation for living life through his absolutes.

"Let's head back to the fountain... I have something I need to show you on the way," he said with a grin.

"What is it?"

"Just wait, you'll see!"

~ *"Everything in this garden is founded on absolutes."* ~

As we passed behind the well, the Gardener unveiled a big row of beautiful watermelons.

"Wow! They're amazing! I had no idea you grew these here!"

"Go ahead, pick out your favorite one!"

Of course, I chose the largest. The Gardener promptly sliced it into long, ruby-red quarters and handed me a piece. I eagerly took an enormous bite and encountered the sweetest, juiciest, most incredible watermelon I think I ever tasted. Without wasting any time, we finished the whole thing!

"Can you believe our clothes are already dry from the heat?" I chuckled after wiping my juicy hands all over my shirt.

"Well, that's only a variable... turn around and look over there!"

The Gardener laughed as he pointed to the late summer sky.

"Oh my... look at those clouds... I guess you're right... the variables *are* always changing!"

A mid-afternoon monsoon rolled in, creating a gentle breeze. Without warning, a blinding flash of lightning zigzagged across the sky, and a loud crack of thunder followed in its wake.

"The rain is coming! Do you want to take shelter, Birdy?"

"How about if we stay right here... I don't care if I get drenched to the core!" I replied as I lifted my hands to the sky.

"Good idea! Let's enjoy every second of it!"

Before we knew it, sheets of rain showered the garden. The cool water ran down our bodies until the clouds emptied themselves of every last drop of water. I closed my eyes for a moment and breathed in the fragrant air left by the deluge.

"Wasn't that simply delicious? Rain showers on a hot summer day are one of my very favorite things in life!"

"I love them too! And do you realize the warmer the day... the more refreshing the cool water *feels*?"

"So, what you're saying is... the horrible heat actually added to this wonderful day!"

"My how quickly things can change! From the worst day... to the best day! And what has changed for you, Birdy?"

"Nothing! The absolutes will never change. They are the same yesterday, today, and forever. The variables may change, but that only happens after I factor in the absolutes first. The rain is gone... but you're still here! And the scorching heat is gone... but you're still here! Even the watermelon's gone... but you're still here! And... if *everything's* gone... you're still here!"

"I AM here, and that is your absolute! I have given absolutely all I AM so you can have absolutely all you will ever need. Everything else is just a variable! And that means you can have a good day every day, can't you?"

"Yes... I can! This garden... is not a product of what it went through or is going through... rather, it's a product of what *you* went through... what *you're* doing to restore it into its absolute destiny. Everything else is just a variable!"

"Yes!" he affirmed with a big sparkling smile as he wrung the rainwater from his cap. "The absolutes of truth are where you will find perfect peace!"

The Gardener gave me a warm bear hug, like I was his little girl.

"Birdy, I will never let you go... that's an absolute!"

I could rest - cherished, safe, and secure!

All was well!

Absolutely perfect!

~ "The absolutes of truth are where you will find perfect peace!" ~

CHAPTER 11

Sea of Forgetfulness

After the Gardener and I spent our precious morning hour together, he opened the garden gate for all to partake of its bounty.

The glorious weather brought in a stream of visitors from all walks of life. Many people simply came to enjoy its beauty while some meandered in to muse and satisfy their curiosity. Young children played in it like a park whereas the elderly enjoyed its solitude and peace. Others sought a friend in hopes to escape their momentary loneliness. And of course, the Gardener always looked forward to meeting each one.

As much as I enjoyed our guests, I dreaded the mess of wrappers, tin cans, and plastic bottles they left behind. Truth is, the sight of any kind of litter unnerved me because it reminded me of my own past failures. Unfortunately, the more people that visited my garden, the bigger the mess seemed to be.

Today I went around as usual with my black trash bag collecting all the rubbish left soiling the grounds. I tried to keep a good attitude but found myself growing increasingly frustrated, and even bitter by everyone's negligence. And though I tried to keep my exasperated feelings to myself, I couldn't conceal them from the Gardener. After we bid farewell to our last guest, he closed the gate and gave me a big grin.

"How are you doing Birdy? Something's been bothering you all day."

"Can you tell?"

"What do you think? You're the only person I know who can walk around in a huff and smile at the same time."

"Was I that obvious? I worked hard to hide my irritation! Truth is... look at this garden... just look at this mess! Why can't people clean up after themselves? How am I supposed to cope with all of this? And the problem is getting worse every day!"

Just then, the Gardener walked into his tool shed and wheeled out a bright blood-red garbage bin.

"I guess I need to deal with my frustration better... but people are not picking up after themselves and believe me, I've hinted in every possible way."

I let out a loud sigh and kicked an empty soda can towards him.

"Yes, I saw some of your 'hints' today," he winked as he picked up the can and discarded it.

"Where did you get this blood-red garbage bin... I've never seen one this color before!"

"Oh, I bought it a long time ago to remove everyone's rubbish."

As I examined it further, I noticed the words *Sea of Forgetfulness* painted on its side in bold navy-blue letters.

"Birdy, why don't you hand me all the trash you collect, and I'll follow right behind you with my *big blood-red bin.*"

"Okay... here's a bunch more wrappers... we've got a lot of work to do."

The Gardener took the litter and immediately disposed of it, never to be remembered again.

But I still remembered!

"Don't *you* ever get irritated by everyone's garbage?" I asked, feeling justified for my self-righteous indignation over the sloppy messes left behind.

"My mission is not to point out everyone's flaws and failures. I don't value or identify people by how they treat this garden."

"Well... what is your mission?"

"My mission is to remove all of the rubbish... and bring wholeness to this garden. People are always going to be messy and careless... that's why I have already prepared a way to remove their failures. Notice that brown lunch bag over there on the park bench beside the fountain? Do you know who left it there?"

I knew the answer because I'd seen it happen every day for the

~ *"People are always going to be messy and careless... that's why I have already prepared a way to remove their failures."* ~

past several months.

"Old Mr. Brown left it... he crumples it up every day at 2:15 p.m. and then gets up and walks away, leaving it there for me to pick up."

"Did you know that his wife died last year and he's lost the will to live? Did you know the only happiness he holds onto in life is seeing your kind smile and enjoying the peace he finds in this garden? Did you know he's completely unaware that he leaves his empty lunch bag crumpled up on the bench?"

The Gardener's concerned look revealed the pain he felt for Mr. Brown.

"Hmm, it's very sad... how long was he married?"

"67 years..."

"Wow, that's a long time! He's such a nice and gentle old man... I want to help him!"

I picked up Mr. Brown's lunch bag and handed it to the Gardener. Suddenly my frustrations vanished under my newfound compassion. Now, instead of being upset about the trash left on the bench, I felt deep sympathy. He became a precious individual who needed to be understood and loved rather than a detriment to my garden.

"Birdy, would you mind bringing me the newspapers laid out underneath the willow tree?"

"'Loopy Lulu' left them... she always does!"

"Well, that's what everyone calls her, but her real name is Talula."

Miss Lulu came to the garden several times a week, carrying her life's belongings in a black garbage bag stuffed in an old rusty grocery cart. Her graying hair laid knotted up in a frizzy bun on the back of her head, held together by its own dirt and secured with an old rubber band. Her tattered clothes and mismatched tennis shoes had gaping holes.

"I wonder why she always lays out herself a bed of newspapers and takes a nap when she visits."

"Do you know her background?"

"Well, I know she looks homeless... that's about it. What's her story?" I asked, knowing the Gardener knew about every person who entered the garden.

"Miss Talula has been homeless for years. When her alcoholic mother died, her dad began to abuse her, until she ran away. Since then, she's lived on the streets trying to protect herself from every kind of crime. Soon after she ran away, someone hit her over the head with a glass bottle. She suffered damage to her brain and became unable to cope with life. Her greatest desire is safety... and this garden has become her safe place. That is why she falls asleep as soon as she gets here. It's the only place where her nightmares cannot invade her dreams."

The Gardener's eyes glistened with tender concern, revealing his deep love for her. Immediately I felt so thankful for the cups of water and fruit we shared with her over the years. She always burst into a toothless smile and nervously took the gifts while muttering incoherent words to herself.

"I wish I could do more for her. Do you think there is any hope for Miss Lulu and Mr. Brown?" I questioned, now feeling the Gardener's heart of empathy.

"Of course there is! Someday soon they will have their own garden. That's why they have come here. No matter what their age is, or their abilities are, they too can have hope for such a garden!" he assured with a confident nod of his head.

"What else can I do for them?"

"You can introduce them to me!"

"That's true... you'll be able to help them!" I agreed as I crumpled up her leftover newspapers.

He quickly disposed of them and gratefully smiled as if I'd done him a big favor. I could tell my simple acts of kindness meant so much to him.

"Birdy, do you know that whatever you do for them, you do for me? When they hurt, I hurt. When you feed them, you feed me. When you welcome them, you welcome me."

"I never realized this!"

"When you love them, you love me! And when you love me, you can love them. And the more you love them... the more you will know my love!"

"That's a lot to take in... but I need this kind of love!"

A transformation began to take place in my thought process as I started to see each guest through the Gardener's eyes. He treasured every person apart from their age, ethnic group, social position, academic status, financial standing, or life accomplishments. None of these things mattered to him, nor did he factor them into his thinking. He saw their value, not their dysfunctions. He gave each person priceless worth and loved them every bit as much as he loved me.

"I guess I can't show them your love unless I am first willing to forgive them for all their offensive behavior."

"Forgiveness is choosing not to remember the offenses of others against you. It renders their wrongs powerless over us. Forgiveness takes hold of the goodness I have given you and passes it on to those in need of it."

"Well, since you've forgiven me... and graced me with your love and honor... I guess this means that I can freely give away all you have already given me!"

"Exactly, Birdy... this kind of love never runs dry!"

Before I knew it, the Gardener and I reminisced about every visitor we met that day. We exchanged creative ideas of how we could encourage and care for each person more effectively. As I began to understand his heart, I realized that I didn't have to look at their litter the same way ever again! It no longer gripped me with self-righteous indignation! The messes that others left behind became just another occasion for me to love each person all the more.

"You know, I never imagined that this unwanted chore I criticized and complained about would grow into a cherished part of my daily routine with you."

The Gardener laughed, "Are you telling me that picking up other

~He saw their value, not their dysfunctions. He gave each person priceless worth and loved them every bit as much as he loved me. ~

people's litter has become..."

"... a privilege!" I interrupted with a chuckle.

"That's exactly how I felt about you!"

The Gardener winked at me and tousled my already-messy hair.

"Do you remember the piles of junk you got rid of when you first cleaned out this garden?"

He didn't answer. He simply grinned, took the trash from my hands and disposed of it.

"When I think about how many times you've picked up my rubbish... and never complained once... I realize how much I've needed a major attitude adjustment... and it got adjusted today. You've taught me how to look past people's litter and see each heart hungering to be nurtured and loved."

"This my dear, is another great key to life!"

"Speaking of litter... here's the last bit of trash.... your *Sea of Forgetfulness* bin is completely stuffed to the top... I'm not sure there's room for anything else!"

"Why don't you have a peek inside."

The Gardener opened the lid for me to get a good look.

"It's empty! It's all gone! Where did all the rubbish go?"

"Into the *Sea of Forgetfulness*!" he grinned.

"Every last bit is gone forever..."

"... never to be remembered again!"

His love showed me a better way!

~ *"Forgiveness is choosing not to remember the offenses of others against you.*

It renders their wrongs powerless over us." ~

CHAPTER 12

The Solution

'Get up! Get up!' screamed the words that awakened me with a startle.

"Who shouted at me... or did I dream it?"

Either way, I needed to get up. Chomping at the bit, I sprung out of bed - my mind flooded with the day's urgent tasks.

"There is so much to do... how am I going to get it all done in time? I'm already feeling overwhelmed!"

Instantly, my 'I can do it' mode kicked in and a burst of adrenaline coursed through my body, propelling me into action. I quickly threw on my clothes, stuffed a piece of dry toast in my mouth, and washed it down with a cup of boiling coffee. Yes, it burned my mouth but work awaited me, and as they say, 'The show must go on!'

Without wasting another second, I rushed out to the garden ready to conquer the busy autumn morning. My mind scrolled through a long list of jobs that needed to be finished before we opened the gate. Plus, the members of the City Botanical Society planned to visit today. The Society consisted of a group of stuffy women that enjoyed looking down their noses at anyone who didn't do things in their prescribed way. Of course, the Gardener did everything unconventionally because he always thought outside the box. And I knew they would disapprove of at least one thing or another by the end of the day. This reality left me anxious and stressed. So, I set out to make the garden look perfect; anything to avoid their formidable reproach.

"Where should I begin?" I groaned as I frantically checked my watch. "Hmm, guess I'll start by raking up the leaves... then I'll empty yesterday's trash into the Gardener's big blood-red bin... I know that's empty! Maybe I can get everything finished before I meet him."

I quickly shifted into high gear and set to work.

Then it all happened!

The blustery wind swooped my pile of raked leaves into the air and scattered them all over the lawn. If that wasn't enough, the gusts tipped over all the trashcans and blew every last bit of litter everywhere.

"Oh no... this isn't good! It's worse than when I began... and the clock's ticking!"

All the while in the back of my mind, I knew I needed to stop and spend my usual morning appointment with the Gardener.

"But he knows we have important people visiting today, and the work must get done before they arrive! It's imperative!" I resolved, trying to justify my actions.

The Gardener's voice suddenly interrupted my complaining.

"Oh, what a beautiful morning... oh, what a beautiful day!" he sang as he walked toward me with his usual delightful smile.

I swallowed hard and kicked the leaves on the ground. What would I tell him? I tried to think of a good excuse for abandoning him, but every explanation seemed to escape me. I knew I had no valid reason except for my own anxious impatience.

"What a pleasure to see you up and about so early, Miss Birdy!"

His face lit up like it always did every morning when he saw me.

In complete guilt, I blurted out, "Uh, hi there... sorry I'm late! You know, we have so much to do... so I thought I'd first rake the leaves and empty the trash before we met up. But the wind ruined all my work, and now it looks... well... pretty bad!"

I hung my head in remorse and nervously sighed. In addition to my already overwhelmed feelings, I now felt distant from the Gardener.

"Birdy, my child... let me see your beautiful face!" he said while gently lifting my chin with his hand.

"Well, everything is just one big mess!"

I tried to avoid his eyes, but he wouldn't let me.

"You don't need to worry. It will all get done at the right time! The weatherman said it would be windy this morning, but it should calm down soon." He paused a moment to carefully choose the right words, "You know Birdy, I don't like to see you strive. We live in a worry-free garden! Every task is already perfectly planned and accounted for. Remember... it's *my* work... all I ask you to do... is join me. Only one thing is needed to prepare your garden for today... that is to take time with me. The work is always easy when we partner together... in fact, everything we accomplish in this garden is the result of teamwork... and we are a team!"

I knew he was right. Why didn't I stop and spend time with him first? None of this would have happened. Completely irritated with myself, I bit the inside of my lip and shook my head. My best intentions self-destructed!

"I guess you should be frustrated with me... sorry I ditched you and tried to fix the garden by myself. I know I failed you... once again... y... you really wouldn't want to spend time with me anyway... at least not now..." I stammered, unable to look at him.

Even though I deserved his displeasure, deep down I longed for things to be right between us.

"Don't ever be afraid of me!" he whispered as his loving eyes met mine. "How do you think I feel about you right now?"

"How *do you feel* about me?"

I studied his face and awaited his disapproval, but as usual, saw nothing but kindness. It seemed the Gardener read my mind once again. With a gentle smile, he took my hand and led me over to a wooden bench in the corner of the garden where he could shelter me from the wind. As we sat down, he put his arm around me and gave me a gentle squeeze.

"Everything's going to be okay!" he whispered.

Why had I feared him? He remained the same wonderful, unchanging Gardener. The gap I felt between us lived in my heart alone. The more I pulled away from him, the more lovingly he pursued me, never allowing a moment of separation.

"Have you eaten from the wrong tree?"

~ *"The work is always easy*
when we partner together." ~

"What do you mean... the wrong tree?"

"There are two trees in this garden. The first one is our relationship tree that will always bear good fruit in your life. The second one is your self-performance tree that causes you to strive to manufacture fruit... but it's all in vain... shame, pride and fear are it's only crop... it's a tree of death!"

"Yeah... I guess I have been eating from the second tree... and I've come up short. I'm so ashamed... I want to hide."

"My dear child... you are basing your view of how I see you on your own actions or lack thereof... *your* performance. My love for you is not dependent on your ability to perform perfectly. Back when you only saw an old abandoned lot... I envisioned the trophy garden that I created it to be. Your validation of this garden, your performance of how you treated it... even your wrong understanding of what it appeared to be, didn't change the reality of your garden's purpose or destiny. My grace alone, my already-determined good plans for your garden... and my unconditional love completed it... because I saw more than dirt. You don't have to perform and prove anything to others through your garden... or manufacture your own fruit... but rather leave it completely surrendered to my care as you did long ago. I didn't create this garden with a bunch of 'to do's' that you must accomplish to be 'good'... you can't manufacture your own goodness. Everything here is born out of our relationship... it's your tree of life."

"So... are you saying that *you* are my tree of life... and the only way to enjoy the fruit is from our relationship?" I asked, still trying to fully grasp what he meant.

"Every bit of fruit in this garden is a product of our relationship. True fruit can't be produced in any other way. It's a partnership of life! If you come to me based on what you alone have or haven't done, you will always lack in some way or another. As I said before, I'm not interested in your ability to perform for me. Rather, I simply desire you to receive all I have already accomplished for you. I have completed everything necessary so you can live from my tree of life!"

"How exactly do I live from this tree of life?"

"You must take hold of all that *my* relationship with you

provides!"

"And how do I do that?"

"Live in *my* presence, and from *my* supply... here you will live from *my* tree of life... where *my* peace and *my* rest will bear lasting fruit!"

The Gardener warmly smiled, once again infusing my heart with hope. I knew this garden's creation had nothing to do with my ability in the first place - the Gardener made all of it. So why did I think my performance would change how he saw or loved me? And why did I think I needed to run ahead of him when he only asked me to receive everything he already accomplished? When I tried to control everything by myself, it resulted in some kind of strife or fiasco. That's why I gave the garden to the Gardener in the first place. How could I forget? How did I end up here again? Where did I get this notion that I needed to make things happen and try to maintain the garden apart from him? Why did I try to perform or impress anyone? Why did I go back to that old lie that kept me from resting in his work alone? He never failed me, and I couldn't remember a time when he lacked anything, nor did I ever see him stressed or in a hurry.

"How did I end up in this pickle?"

The Gardener rubbed his chin like he did when he needed to say something important.

"Every time you try to assume ownership of the garden... you single-handedly take on the full responsibility of its maintenance... this means the complete burden of its provision and protection falls on your shoulders alone!"

"Hmm... this is what happened! I trusted in my *own* feeble ability to control and fix circumstances... what a mistake!"

"Yes... and it's from *this* mindset, you try to manufacture your *own* good fruit. This is a problem... because when you are unable to fulfill each need due to your *own* limitations... your perspective and motivation become rooted in fear... and when you fail... you feel ashamed."

"I know... during these times, I see every need as a threat... then I become fearful... which puts me in survival mode... and I either freak out or melt down!"

"Yes Birdy, fear pushes you to control and fix your problems... or causes you to run and hide."

"Yeah... either way... I end up even more stressed!"

"It's a dark circle of fear that will make you spiral into a pit of despair."

"Well... how am I supposed to succeed in a world full of problems?"

"Your fight is not against issues or problems. When every pressing need screams at you, your only fight is to believe that *my* ability and *my* work is always enough. It's a good fight of faith that chooses to trust me above everything else. If you need your circumstances perfectly aligned and in place to be at peace... you become a product of them and are only as good as they dictate. If they are good, you are good, and if they are not good, neither are you. The problem is, they have no power to give life. Instead, they bind you with life-choking fear. You must put your trust in the only *Solution* who is greater than your circumstances. No burden is a problem for me. I don't see troubles apart from their solutions... and problems are just another opportunity to display all *I AM*. Remember long ago... when you released your garden to me and gave me full ownership? Well, you must continue to trust *my* complete ability to guard and provide for it. When you do, your perspective and motivation will be rooted in *my* love. It's a faith that works by love. As you give your burdens to me and trust in *my* love, you will be able to rest in faith... and never fear any lack again... even in the worst circumstances."

"You make it sound so simple! I guess you only see possibilities when my calculations are riddled with impossibilities. I know in my head that you've already accomplished everything that concerns me. Now I need to continually see my life from your perspective and allow you to author my reality... and then... remind myself of these truths when the confusion starts next time!"

"You're right! You got it! In this garden, we never start with the problem... instead, we always begin with the *Solution!* Birdy, I AM the Gardener of this garden... *The Solution* to every need here. Your part is to believe that everything I have done and promised to do for you is entirely accurate. Listen to my voice alone... base your every response and action on the truth of *my* promises... even though you may not physically see them.... here you will find true rest."

"I remember the first time I surrendered this garden to you... what rest I felt. The burden lifted from my shoulders and the stress disappeared. It's all about our relationship, isn't it?" I concluded, now aware that all my problems started when I tried to fix everything on my own.

"Yep! It goes back to living in partnership with me... partaking from *my* tree of life. My presence does not need or desire your performance, only your attendance!" the Gardener tenderly, but adamantly stated.

"It's so simple... just being with *you*... that's where true fruit is born! No more eating from my performance tree... no more running ahead of you... like I did earlier today. You have faithfully accomplished everything necessary to complete what you began in this garden years ago. The driving voice of fear that awoke me this morning and rushed me into the day was a lie. Never again will I let these lies cause me to be anxious. Those days of feeling like I alone am fighting against time, circumstances, and sometimes people... are finally over!"

The Gardener grinned and gave me a big affirmative nod. I no longer cared if the Mayor himself visited the garden, much less the women from the City Botanical Society. No, I wouldn't let them bully me because I didn't fit into their club. Nor would I be intimidated if they tried to impose their pompous old traditions and rules on my garden. I would not permit myself to listen to their burdensome comments nor worry about their pointless dogmas. I could rest in the Gardener's care alone.

~ *"My presence does not need or desire your performance, only your attendance!"* ~

"It's going to be a good day today! Expect it to be!" he whispered as he put his arm around me.

Every last anxious thought that woke me up this morning disappeared into the reality of his wonderful truth. The turbulent storm inside me, along with the boisterous winds outside, settled into a quiet stillness. My garden returned to its perfect, sweet serenity.

"I think it's time to get to work!" the Gardener said handing me a rake. "Here's the plan... you rake up all the leaves, and we'll get the job done together."

I immediately set to my task, but this time a tranquil peace filled the garden. While whistling his favorite tune, my *Solution* walked up and parked his wheelbarrow next to the pile of leaves I gathered. Before I knew it, we tucked every loose leaf into the compost bin.

"What about the trash?"

"It's done!"

"How about all the other chores?"

"All the work's finished! The only thing left to do is open the front gate!"

"Wow! How did you get everything done so fast?"

"Remember, I AM the garden's Keeper! It's amazing how quickly things get done when we work together!"

The Gardener winked at me and took my rake to put back in the shed. We both glanced over the garden once more. It looked pristine and inviting in every way. Peace settled in my heart not because everything lined up in perfect order, but because I knew I could trust my Gardener. Faith enabled me to see beyond my difficulties and problems to *The Solution*!

I found his perfect rest.

"...my Gardener... my *Solution*... my Absolute... my Tree of Life!"

CHAPTER 13

Hume

"What time is it?" I said as I looked at my alarm clock. "Oh no... it's still the wee hours of the morning! The wind howled all night long... I don't think I slept a wink!"

I adjusted my pillow and snuggled down under the blankets. But the roaring wind continued to whistle through the cracks in my house, and I couldn't get back to sleep.

"Well... I'm fully awake now... I might as well get up and be productive!"

I promptly threw together a batch of apple muffins to share with the Gardener. As soon as they finished baking, I placed them in my basket next to a freshly brewed pot of tea and covered them with a linen cloth. After putting on my thickest sweater and old windbreaker, I set out for the garden. The fierce wind pressed against me, making it difficult to close the gate.

"You nasty piece of dirt... you'll never amount to anything," shouted a harsh voice out of nowhere.

His scathing words grew louder by the minute, filled with accusations that reminded me of my past. I looked around to identify who yelled but saw no one. Where did this guy come from? What did he want? He appeared to know every sensitive trigger inside me and intentionally used specific language to upset me. I glanced over the garden gate again hoping to find the source of the profane arrows. Suddenly a bunch of little stones pelted my face.

"Ouch!" I yelped, jumping back. "What hit me? That really hurt!"

I quickly gathered up what looked like small dirt clods filled with seeds and stuffed them in my coat pocket to show the Gardener.

The vile shouts continued. Who would do this? Why me? What were these seeds? Again, I looked for clues but found nothing.

As I stood up, a gust of wind just about knocked me over. My hair blew in my mouth, and my eyes stung from all the dust encircling me. At the same time, my mind began to flood with old memories of this once-desolate field that had now become my garden. The nasty bite in the air left me startled with a dark, momentary déjà vu. Even the wind kicked up in the same miserable way, challenging everything I believed.

"I'm not going there for a moment!" I called out as I tried to shake off the morning events. "No way... I choose not to be bothered by the wind, nor will I waste my time reminiscing unwanted memories. I have something much better ahead. The Gardener awaits me with new hope... just like he has every single day!"

"Good morning!" greeted a kind, familiar voice behind me.

"Oh, it's you... I'm sure glad to see you. And if you say it's a good morning... then good morning to you, too!" I replied, picking up my basket.

"Are you okay, Birdy?"

"Well... yeah... kinda!"

"Come with me."

The Gardener put his hand on my shoulder and quickly ushered me into the greenhouse.

"We need a shelter today, so let's sit in here."

Instantly, a quiet calm hushed the residue left by the haunting screams. I sat down on a wooden stool next to the Gardener and handed him an apple muffin.

"Thank you! This tastes delicious!"

His face lit up with a smile that seemed to put some normalcy back into my day.

"I'm so sorry these muffins are cold... they should still be warm... but I encountered a problem when I entered the garden this morning."

"So what happened, my dear?" he asked while pouring me a hot cup of tea.

"I'm not sure what just happened... but as I closed the gate

~ *"The Gardener awaits me with new hope...*
just like he has every single day!" ~

behind me, I heard someone yell hurtful words that triggered dark thoughts from my past. When I looked up to see where it came from, little dirt clods filled with seeds hit my face."

"Can I see them?"

"Sure, here they are..."

I reached into my pocket, pulled out the round clumps, and handed them to the Gardener.

"It's so bizarre! They seemed to fly right over the top of the garden wall. Do you know what kind of seeds they are?" I asked, still trying to solve the mysterious events of the morning.

The Gardener crushed the dirt between his fingers and carefully examined the seeds.

"Hmm," he furrowed his brow and shook his head. "I think I have an explanation... yep, just what I thought... these clumps are weed seeds. They are from the enemy, alright! He is trying to sow weeds in your garden."

"What kind of weeds?"

"Oh... looks like Bindweed, Horsetail, and Couch grass seeds. They're all dangerous. These kinds of weeds don't initially look threatening, but they will hinder your garden from thriving. They sprout up overnight and rob both space and nutrients from everything else. They're very destructive... and can be difficult to get rid of. Do you remember when we first began to remove the weeds?"

"Yeah... we threw every last one of them in the fire!"

The Gardener looked at the seeds once again.

"We have an enemy who wants to resow these into your garden. But... that's not going to happen! We aren't going to allow any of them to creep back in!" he assured with an authoritative resolve.

"Amen! And I'm not going to allow those nasty words he screamed to take root in my thoughts, either. At first, my mind started to relive the lying memories... but I immediately resolved not to partner with them... not even for a moment! They are nothing more than dark weeds that have no place in my garden... and they have no right to come back... ever again!" I adamantly concluded, trying to preach truth to myself in the process.

"Absolutely, Birdy! Don't give them a second of your time. The enemy hurled them at you with one intention, and that's to destroy!"

Then all at once, he took the rest of the seeds and dumped them in the garbage bin.

"Well, what if there are more that I missed?"

"Did you notice the wind?"

"Yes... how could I not?"

"Our enemy threw these seeds over your garden wall hoping to plant them inside. But the only seeds that landed in the garden were the ones that fell around you. The rest never made it... thanks to the wind!"

"Wait, were you there?"

"Remember, I make it my business to know *everything* that goes on in this garden!"

"I guess I should be thankful for the wind... no matter how cold or blustery it feels. Our enemy does not like this garden, does he?"

"No, he does not! He has tried to ruin every inch of it from day one... but he cannot!"

I could tell the enemy's futile attempt to sabotage my garden did not threaten the Gardener. *His* confidence gave *me* confidence.

"Well, all those fearful shouts I heard this morning have been captured and officially disposed of too."

The Gardener winked and gave me a big 'well done' grin. I sat silent for a few moments and reflected on the old truths I'd read in my big brown leather folder.

"Will you tell me the story of my garden again? I never get tired of hearing you share it. Besides, it's too windy to work outside... we might as well make good use of our time... pleeease?"

I knew full well the Gardener would fulfill my heart's desire.

He smiled at my request and began, "Many, many years ago, I decided to create a garden... not any ordinary garden, but one that would look like my own... one that I could lovingly care for and tend with my own hands. So, I made a world that actually began as a big garden itself. It flourished with every kind of life. Now, in this new world, I made a smaller garden... a true paradise. But I did not stop there! Inside this smaller garden, I made a third garden. However, this garden was different than all the others. I created this garden to house my seeds of life. It would look just like me. So, I took the richest, finest 'hume,' which means soil, and I began to form it into a perfect garden. Once I cultivated the soil, I breathed my very own seed of life into it, and the first 'hume-man' garden grew with my glorious likeness. Yes... he was *very good* in every way! From that day forward, I personally tended his growth, and nourished him as my child. I even created a wife for him out of his very substance so they could share life in the garden with me. But... the story does not end there. One day my enemy, the old serpent himself, came to the 'hume-mans' with a plan to destroy them. Because the serpent hated me, he hated them as well. He then set out to seduce the 'hume-man' and his wife into eating fruit from the tree of death that I forbade them to partake of. Unfortunately, his plan to deceive them worked. Forsaking my advice, they consumed the forbidden fruit... seeds and all. What a terrible day! The serpent buried his death seeds in their soil, swiftly killing all the life in their gardens. They looked like an exposed wasteland of naked dirt. In shame, the 'hume-mans' frantically placed fig leaves all over their gardens and hid from me. They hoped to somehow make themselves look like the glorious gardens I originally created them to be... but of course... they couldn't."

The Gardener hesitated, looked down at the ground and shook his head before he continued.

"Yes, my precious gardens lost their 'very good' that day! I couldn't look upon their devastation and wreckage... but that was not the end. Even though the enemy thought he killed all 'hume-manity's' gardens... he *didn't* know I had a perfect plan already in place. I would once again become their Gardener and restore their gardens with *my* life. So, with all that I AM, and in full knowledge it would cost me my very life... I set out to destroy the curse of the death seeds. I then became a 'hume-man' garden myself and chose to live among 'hume-manity's' debris. My garden looked perfect, void of a single weed. It flourished with life, which I continually gave away to every lost and ruined garden I encountered. I loved their

~ "Even though the enemy thought he killed all 'hume-manity's' gardens... he didn't know I had a perfect plan already in place. I would once again become their Gardener and restore their gardens with my life." ~

146

gardens... seeing the devastation and wreckage broke my heart, because I knew what I created them to be. Yet even though I shared my garden's beautiful life with them, they rejected me and demolished my garden with their death. I will never forget that day... I allowed them to destroy my garden with all 'hume-manity's' weedy filth and ruin. They piled every bit of their evil seeds and destructive thistles into my garden until it died."

The Gardener stopped for a moment and passionately looked at his scarred hands. My eyes teared up as he lovingly showed me the marks on his palms.

"This is where your scars came from... isn't it?"

"Yes... these scars are the result of removing the filth from every person's garden. I have no regrets though, and never will. Because now I AM able to restore every single 'hume-man' into the garden they are meant to be. You see, when my garden died, it could not stay dead. The life in my garden was more powerful than the death in everyone else's!"

His eyes lit up with enthusiasm as he spoke. I loved happy endings and couldn't wait for him to get to the victorious grand finale! So, in my overzealous excitement, I jumped ahead and finished his story.

"That means that you have the power to transform every 'hume-man' plot into the perfect garden you first destined them to become... and that means every single person has a garden awaiting them!"

The Gardener's twinkle suddenly disappeared, and his tone became somber, "They do, but most of them don't know a garden awaits them. They need to hear the Good News and receive the garden that I purchased for them."

"And then allow you to be their Gardener... just like I did!"

"They don't understand that I AM the only Gardener who carries the life needed to resurrect their gardens... no one else can do my job."

"Well... they need to know the truth... and I will tell them! Why wouldn't they want to know? It's a no-brainer! All they have to do is look at what you have done with my garden... it's a glorious

~ "They don't understand that I AM the only Gardener who carries the life needed to resurrect their gardens... no one else can do my job." ~

testimony of your ability... and I love every part of it!"

"What do you love most, Birdy?"

"You're here! You're the Father of this garden... and everything in it is the essence of your overflowing love. This is your original creation. You rescued it after being trafficked by your enemy. I will never forget that first day when you met me here and began to re-create it with your seeds of life. Your restoration is, in reality, my salvation... it's where I meet you. It's my safe place where I find peace and where your truth renews me... where I am fully alive. It's where I have come to know you, and knowing you is the very reason I live. It's where I have learned to hear your voice and follow as you lead me. It's also where all who enter can taste and see your beauty... and where many will meet you for the first time."

I stopped to reflect for a moment and went on.

"You know... I especially love to offer the fountain's cool water to all our thirsty guests. And I love watching their eyes light up when they taste it and see how good it is... and then I love to tell them... drink as much as you want... it's all free! I love when people stop to smell the delicious flowers. I love to help them pick fruit and see their faces when they bite into a juicy peach or pear. I love to watch the children chasing the bunnies as the elderly sit on the benches and observe the birds. I love to see young people gaze at their reflections in the pond and watch their surprised smiles when they are graced with a school of colorful fish. I love when each person personally meets you. I love to see you reach out and touch them with your love... I know they will never be the same. In fact, it is only a matter of time until their gardens become beautiful as well. You love taking their ruined plots of earth and creating a paradise... don't you?"

The Gardener smiled tenderly and nodded. His gentle gaze reached into the very depths of my soul.

"But what I love most... is that I am yours..."

"... and you are mine... for eternity!"

"My garden belongs to you and you're the Master... this is your Kingdom... and you are my King!"

"It's why I came! My greatest delight is... to dwell with you, Birdy!"

"Thank you, thank you, thank you, thank you... each time you tell me the story of my garden... I see the big picture and I grow more and more in awe of you! It reminds me of why I believe what I believe... and makes me forever indebted to you!"

The Gardener grinned and replied, "Always live in what you believe, rather than believe in what you live."

"Pardon me... can you repeat that? I need to hear it again..."

Slowing down, he repeated, "Always live in what you believe, rather than believe in what you live." He must have noticed the blank look on my face, so he continued to elaborate, "Live from the truth of who I AM and what I've created you and your garden to be. Believe and live in this truth every single moment of every single day. Live in the truth of what I've already accomplished. This means you must not allow what life hurls in your path to speak louder than truth. And certainly do not let any of those bad seeds take root in your garden. Step into everything I paid for and live from *this* place alone."

The Gardener awaited my response to see if I understood.

"Live... in what you believe... don't believe... in what you live. Yes, I am getting it now... I need to let the truth of who *you* are and what *you've* done, be what I believe above all. Then it will become the lens that I view my life through. I must not be deceived or defined by my past life... nor allow it to dictate my present thoughts or actions... especially since you have given me a beautiful new life. I must constantly remember the story of my garden, this helps me see who I am and how I should respond... no matter what life throws at

149

me... did I get it?"

"You've got it!"

The Gardener grinned from ear to ear, letting me know that I successfully understood another one of his keys for life.

By now, the winds scattered the clouds, and the sun warmed the greenhouse with its radiant light.

"Shall we go outside? Here, let me get the door for you... ladies first!"

The whole garden glistened with vibrancy and spoke of his love for me.

"What a turn of events we've had today! It started out yucky... but once again, you reminded me... I can trust your truth above all."

"Living what you believe not only removes the enemy's power to sow his seeds in your garden... but also empowers you to share your story with all who come to visit. Speaking of visitors... I think it's time to open the garden's gate... are you ready, my dear?"

"Yes, I'm ready... and what a beautiful sunny day it's turned into! The sky is sooo blue! You do all things well! I never grow tired of your creation. It speaks of you and tells your story of love everywhere it blooms. It is sooo good!" I whispered as my eyes savored the paradise that lay before me.

"Indeed, it *is* VERY, VERY GOOD!" the Gardener triumphantly beamed.

~ *"Always live in what you believe, rather than believe in what you live."* ~

CHAPTER 14

Winter Song

Gently awakened by the warm sunlight that streamed through my window, I peeked open one eye.

The weather looked promising, so I eagerly jumped out of bed. By the time I left my house, however, black billowing clouds melted away the morning sun. They vigorously delivered raging winds that howled like a pack of hungry wolves.

"Goodbye, autumn! I'm going to miss you... and hello winter... I'm not very excited that you're here!"

A frigid chill pierced through my body as I entered the garden. Within minutes, sheets of rain dropped from the sky, soaking me from head to toe. The Gardener saw my plight and quickly gave me his coat.

"Let's head for the gazebo. It's the closest shelter for now."

"Where did this storm come from? Looks pretty bad!"

"Yes, it looks that way... but every day in the garden is good!" Then leaning in closer, he lowered his voice and asked, "Birdy, do you trust me?"

"Of course, I do!"

"Remember, don't let your outside circumstances dictate your inside perspective. Trust *me*... it's your place of peace... and always know... this too shall pass!"

I wasn't quite sure what he meant, but I knew I could trust him, so I gave him a big nod.

Before I knew it, the Gardener invited every person needing shelter to join us under the gazebo. Stuck inside, we crowded together like sardines, and silently waited for the crazy weather to subside. Instead, the pelting downpour intensified to the point that everyone thought the roof might cave in. I didn't think it would though; the Gardener built it, and whatever he did lasted forever.

After about an hour, the rain began to let up, and we all breathed a big sigh of relief. Well, that is for a moment until the clouds abruptly exploded. This time it escalated into torrents of rain and sleet. Every face drooped in disappointment. Hope deferred made their hearts sick. The group huddled closer together trying to stay warm, but no one escaped the frigid wind.

"This is a miserable day!" whined one woman.

"I should have stayed in bed!" agreed another.

"Yes, it's horrible!" yelled a young man.

People began to swear at me as if I created the harsh uncontrollable weather. Suddenly, the wind picked up again, sending a bitter shiver down my already-freezing cold spine. It rushed past every person under the little roof, leaving behind a dissonant chorus of complaining - especially from those who looked for someone to blame for their misfortune.

"How dare this happen to me!" one grumpy old man muttered as he zipped up his coat and yanked his hood over his head.

Everyone seemed upset except for the Gardener. He stood carefully shielding the little ones from the rain which made me so proud of him.

"Thank you!" I quietly mouthed.

I gave him a big smile and he winked at me. His eyes reminded me not to fear the storm but simply wait for it to pass. I knew he had a plan and purpose for every storm. 'They're all part of the various seasons of life,' he would say.

"Why don't we just relax and enjoy the rain?" I suggested.

"Oh yeah, like *that's* gonna help!" bellowed one of the ladies next to me.

"If this rain doesn't stop, I am going to sue you!" threatened the grumpy old man.

What a ridiculous idea! I didn't have anything to do with the rain or freezing temperature, so why did he think he could sue me? I wasn't the culprit! I wanted the rain to stop as much as he did.

~I knew he had a plan and purpose for every storm. ~

"Don't you own this garden?" the old man snarled.

"Well, it belongs to the Gardener," I responded.

"Then it's all his fault! It's always his fault!" he roared.

Seriously, what did any of this have to do with the Gardener? Especially since he built the gazebo that provided a haven for us! It could've been much more devastating without it! Yet I didn't hear anyone thank him. They were too busy playing the victim card and throwing a pity party over their day's hardship. The Gardener, however, stood silently. He could have kicked every last person out into the storm. But that was not his way. People's bad attitudes never changed him for the worse - he always changed them for the better.

Just then, a freezing wind raged through the open sides, making the temperature drop another ten degrees.

"Let's try to huddle closer together so we can keep warm," I said in a feeble attempt to calm the angry voices around me.

"That's fine for you to say since you're already soaking wet. There's no way we're going to get any closer to you!" the lady next to me shrilled.

"You just want to warm yourself up at our expense," scowled another angry person.

I didn't respond to their accusations and saw no need to argue. They looked cold and frazzled and wanted to take out their frustrations on someone.

By now, the sleet turned into hail, which pounded so loudly on the tin roof we could barely hear ourselves talk. Once again, the wind changed direction. The penny-sized ice balls came through the side of the gazebo and pummeled my back. I drew towards the shelter's center, only to be shoved in the ribs by someone's elbow.

The Gardener saw my distress and stepped in front of me and let the hail strike him instead.

Meanwhile, the garden patiently took a beating as the sky unleashed its fury. Sadly, the raging storm crushed all the cyclamen and hellebores, leaving their petals scattered everywhere. The last of autumn's apples lay bruised and battered by the white marbles of ice covering every inch of the ground. Most of the trees suffered damage of one sort or another. The fierce winds stripped away any remaining leaves and broke off most of their limbs. It even flipped the swing upside down and knocked over the arbors that held the grapevines. The whole garden endured such an intense blow, I wondered how it would ever recover from the fallout.

Everyone looked so cold, cranky, and miserable that I wasn't sure I wanted to open my mouth again lest I get severely chastised. Part of me wanted to be a victim of the storm's dark tidings and succumb to the crowd's despairing disposition. But when I looked up, I caught the Gardener peacefully smiling. His eyes comforted me, and he gently squeezed my hand. He didn't seem one bit bothered by the storm or the nasty attitudes loitering in our gazebo. Knowing him, he probably enjoyed the whole ordeal. He always said, 'Life's filled with many storms... never fear them. The bleaker the storm, the greater the triumph!'

Then with a gentle nudge, he leaned over and whispered in my ear, "Sing!"

"Sing?"

Suddenly it dawned on me. Of course! That was it! If he said to sing, then I would sing, no matter what everyone else wanted. Even in the most difficult times, the Gardener's directives were always good. After all, he owned the garden and I could stand confidently in his authority.

Without any hesitation, I opened my mouth and began to sing my favorite song with all my heart. I sang at the top of my lungs in order to hear myself above the hammering hail. No, I wouldn't call it my best day. It didn't feel good to be falsely accused, elbowed in the rib, scolded, put down or freezing cold. And it wasn't easy to see my garden ravaged by the storm either. Yes, I suffered through the day,

154

~If he said to sing, then I would sing, no matter what everyone else wanted. Even in the most difficult times, the Gardener's directives were always good. ~

but I had a greater cause to be happy about. Nothing could take that joy away from me. I chose to be a victor, not a victim. I would endure in triumph and wait for the blessing that always followed. My Gardener had seen many a tempest come and go and overcame each one. He knew my garden back when every storm of life completely destroyed it, yet he stood undaunted by its condition. Why should this turbulence bother him now? It didn't! He seemed entirely above it. If he withstood, I could withstand.

So, I decided I wouldn't focus on this here-and-now trial or let it upset me in any way. How could I let this weather, or anything else for that matter, speak louder than his already-proven love? His truth remained my absolute throughout the storm. And with all eyes on me I continued to sing with my hands raised, not troubled by what anyone else might think. I followed the directive of only One, the Gardener.

As I sang, people began to snicker and murmur, but I couldn't hear what they said. By now, my soul beamed with radiant joy that bubbled over into my song. Had anything changed? No, it hadn't! My Gardener's perspective became my place of peace.

As quickly as the storm appeared, it subsided. The wind died down and the hail sputtered until it finally stopped. Everyone stood speechless and weather-beaten under the gazebo, not sure what to do next. Would there be an aftermath?

Our questions disappeared when the sun broke through the clouds. The snowy hail instantly melted into little puddles of water.

One by one, each person stepped out of the gazebo and began to leave the garden. Many thanked me for allowing them refuge during the storm. One lady even thanked me for the song of hope I sang - she said it brightened her day. Finally, the grumpy older man slowly walked out of the gazebo. We could barely see his face shrouded under his hood. But as he shuffled past us, a strong odor of alcohol lingered in the air. He hung his head low, obviously a bit embarrassed by his nastiness. Either way, I shrugged it off. I felt sorry for the old guy. 'It never hurts to be nice,' I thought, as I gave him the kindest smile I could.

"Please come again anytime!" I called as he walked out the gate.

For a moment, I wondered if I really wanted to see him again, but I quickly decided that I did. After the last visitor left, I stopped to examine the broken state of my garden. Ruin and rubble lay before me. The damage looked a lot worse than I realized. Although, before I could assess the whole situation, I felt the Gardener's hands on my shoulders. He turned me around so I could only see his face.

"Birdy, do you trust me?"

"I do."

"Well... do you want the good news or the bad news first?"

"Tell me the bad news first."

"The garden has been hit quite hard today and will take some time to restore."

"Yeah, I know... it looks pretty beat up," I said glancing over at the wreckage.

Once again, the Gardener drew my eyes back to his own.

"Do you *still* trust me?"

"Y... yes... I do!"

"Now for the good news..." he confidently smiled. "When you fully trust me, you will see me take the broken and make it into something beautiful."

"I guess that's all that matters! I don't know how I would have weathered this trial otherwise... you calm my every storm. And you always have a plan!"

I let out a big sigh as the turbulence from the day dwindled into complete stillness. The sweet fragrances released by the winds smelled delicious and the warmth of the sun began to dry our wet clothes. The Gardener's relaxed demeanor assured me all was well. His hope ruled my heart through the entire storm, and I could stand in full joy.

"Birdy, look at the garden, it's bursting with hope!"

"What are you going to do with it?"

Without giving me an answer, he surveyed the brokenness and grinned. His eyes sparkled with vision of new possibilities which said it all.

"You don't have to answer... I know you already have a miraculous plan to bring life out of what looks like death. It's your way!"

"It will not only look beautiful when it's finished... but we're going to enjoy the ride getting there!" he affirmed.

"Speaking of riding out the storm... I'm so glad you reminded me to trust you this morning. It gave me the sweet peace I needed throughout the whole ordeal! Once upon a time, I would've become so upset and hurt by everything that happened. And I would've given that grumpy old guy a good telling off. But when I saw that you didn't seem the least bit bothered by the whole situation, I rested."

"Well done, Birdy! You weathered this storm like a champion!"

"It definitely challenged me... yet for some strange reason, I'm not tired."

"That's good to hear, because you sure took quite a beating from everyone!"

"Yes, especially from Mr. Grouchy... whoever he is! I wonder if we'll ever see him again?"

"We probably will someday," the Gardener answered with a

~ *"I know you already have a miraculous plan to bring life out of what looks like death. It's your way!"* ~

twinkle in his eye.

"To be honest, I battled to trust you at first... until you encouraged me to sing! Once I sang, the battle disappeared."

He put his arm around me and grinned, "We don't fear the battles... we rest in victory! We have much to sing about because all storms are opportunities to trust *me* even more... they are adventures that always end in triumph!"

"That seems to be the way things go around here!"

A restful silence hovered over the garden. That is, until I looked up at the sky.

"Oh my! What is that?" I exclaimed.

As quickly as the sun came out, the sky darkened, and thick clouds rolled in once again.

Undaunted by the thought of more bad weather, I lightheartedly laughed, "I wonder what the clouds plan to deliver this time? Will it be rain... sleet... hail... wind... or...?"

Before I could finish my sentence, a wet sensation christened my nose.

"Look! It's snowing! I love snow! It's sooo beautiful." I whispered in awe.

We both watched the fluffy flakes silently flutter down to earth. Within minutes, the whole garden lay hidden under soft, powdery snowdrifts, transforming it into a winter wonderland.

"Do you want to make a snow angel?" the Gardener asked.

"Yes! But you go first!"

The Gardener laid on the ground and carved out a perfect angel.

"What do you think?"

"Look at that! It's flawlessly designed! And it looks like fun!" I giggled, watching a grown man flap his arms and legs in the snow.

"Well, I have to admit, it's not the first angel I've ever created," he smiled with a wink.

I playfully plopped on the ground, eager to join him in his winter artwork. I don't know how many angels we made before we found ourselves dusted in white snowflakes from head to toe.

"You know, we could make a snowman, but I think we're both pretty wet and cold."

"I have an idea! Would you like to visit my winter chalet for a cup of hot chocolate and warm yourself by the fire?" he asked, pointing to his small cabin nearby.

"That would be great! I'd love to!"

I never missed an opportunity to enjoy his hospitality. The inside of his cabin looked just like him - charming, clean and timeless. He kept it simple because he spent most of his days out in the garden.

"Do you mind if I dry my coat and socks next to the woodstove?"

"That's what it's there for!" the Gardener smiled as he handed me a cup of his famous cocoa and marshmallows.

"Thanks! Your hot chocolate is the best! What a perfect ending to a great day!"

The Gardener nodded and threw another log on the crackling fire.

"Birdy, look out the window... see how beautiful the garden looks now?"

"Wow... it's breathtaking! You use everything for my *very good* and make everything beautiful in your right time, don't you?"

"Yes... all storms carry a blessing with them!"

"I think we are enjoying that blessing right now."

"A precious blessing indeed!" he beamed.

The Gardener was my Gardener. He never missed an opportunity to manifest his faithfulness and glory, and today's adversity was no exception.

Truly, I could trust him! Could it get any better than this? I could rest.

Need I say more?

The cold, bitter winter felt like it would never end, so when March

~ *"All storms are opportunities*

to trust me even more...

they are adventures that always

end in triumph!" ~

CHAPTER 15

Waiting On The Gardener

came in like a lamb, a hint of hope entered my heart. The weather remained warm and sunny for about a week until the lamb turned into a lion that roared fiercely throughout the remainder of the month.

When April arrived, I thought it would usher in highlights of summer's warmth. But instead of gentle showers, it began with torrential floods that soaked the garden to its core. It rained and rained and rained some more. Waterlogged and without any sunshine in sight, I struggled to keep a good attitude.

Each morning seemed to be a repeat of the day before. I routinely dressed in my wool sweater, oversized raincoat, and yellow wellies before I headed out to the greenhouse to meet the Gardener. Safely sheltered from the downpour, we sat and visited, waiting for the deluge to subside.

Today was no exception.

"Will this rain *ever* stop?" I shouted.

My voice drowned into silence under the pelting drops that clattered against the glass roof. But the Gardener clearly heard me, and I already knew what he would say. He smiled cheerfully, gave me a nod, and we both mouthed the word 'wait' at the same time. He understood how much I struggled to wait for anything, especially with no end in sight. After a while, the rain let up a bit, making it easier to talk and hear one another.

"How are you doing today, my little wet Birdy?

"I'm finished with this rain... seriously!"

The Gardener could see my frustration and gently laid his hand on my shoulder.

"My dear, rest assured when you wait patiently, you will see an abundant increase! Remember, my good plans are neither early nor late... but always arrive right on time! Will you wait with me?"

He didn't seem the least bit troubled or in a hurry and honestly, I envied his peace.

"I guess I have no choice but to wait... I can't stop the rain!"

The Gardener grinned in amusement and began to explain, "What I mean, is will you wait on *me*... look to *me* and trust *my* perfect timing?"

I sat silent for a few seconds trying to resolve my internal battle with truth.

"Do you mean I'm supposed to wait on you and not the circumstances?"

"Well, have I ever let you down?"

"Not that I can think of... you always seem to know what you are doing... and that alone should be enough for me... but doesn't this never-ending rain bother you?"

"No, not one bit!"

"I guess if you're not bothered by the weather, then I shouldn't be either!"

"Birdy... waiting becomes easy when you know I have a plan... and this is all a part of the process!"

"I see... I need to rest in your process, don't I?"

"Yes, trust in what I AM accomplishing during this time!"

"Hmm... I suppose I've been waiting on the rain... and not on you! Okay... from this point forward, I Birdy, choose to wait on *you* above all else!" I triumphantly announced.

"Do you want me to hold you to this?" the Gardener smiled with a wink.

"Yes, I need accountability, especially when my attitude begins to match the weather!" I laughed.

Rainy day after rainy day, we sat together in the glass shelter until that eventful lunchtime when we heard the rattling of someone knocking on the window.

"Hello?" called the pitiful cry from outside.

I opened the greenhouse door and found a young man I'd never seen before standing in front of me. The poor guy looked drenched to the core. His grungy flannel shirt and ripped jeans were thoroughly soaked. Even his backpack dripped with water.

"Would you mind if I came in and got out of this downpour for a bit?" pleaded the stranger.

"Sure, come on in and join us... you look pretty wet!" I replied.

He quickly responded to our invitation. Before we knew it, he dumped his backpack in the driest spot he could find and took off his wet shirt. I felt sorry for him as he stood shivering in his t-shirt. He appeared cold, hungry and worn out. I immediately gave him my oversized raincoat, hoping it would warm him up. It didn't quite fit him, but it would suffice for now.

"What are you doing outside on a day like today?" I inquired as I poured him a hot cup of coffee from the Gardener's thermos.

"Walkin'... just walkin'..." he reluctantly responded.

It seemed there was more to his story, but he wasn't about to divulge it.

"Are you hungry?" the Gardener asked.

The stranger nodded 'yes.' With that, the Gardener laid out his plaid blanket and unpacked the lunch he'd prepared.

"We were just getting ready to eat. Would you like to join us? Have a seat!"

Without a word, the young man sat down and eagerly accepted half of the Gardener's sandwich and half of mine. He gobbled it down in seconds as if he hadn't eaten all week. The Gardener and I exchanged glances and silently agreed that we would give him the rest of our lunch. We could tell he needed it more than we did. No one spoke while our guest devoured every crumb. After he finished, he nodded a quick 'thank you.'

Wanting to break the awkward silence, I mustered up the courage to ask him his name.

"Trav," he answered.

"Travis?" I repeated.

"No... Trav!" he corrected.

With no further explanation, he continued to drink his coffee

~ *"Remember, my good plans*
are neither early nor late…
but always arrive right on time!
Will you wait with me?" ~

right down to the last drop. 'Interesting name,' I thought, as I glanced at the Gardener and raised my eyebrows. He simply smiled a calm, peaceful smile that let me know all was going as planned.

The three of us sat quietly for the rest of the day. This Trav guy obviously didn't want to talk, so instead, the Gardener and I acknowledged our unspoken thoughts to one another. As the evening approached, the stranger emptied his backpack. Then without asking permission, he set up his tent right in the center of my greenhouse.

'Well, what am I supposed to do now?' I wondered as I stared at the makeshift campsite. I bit my lip and looked at the Gardener, hoping he would provide some direction. He simply grinned as though he enjoyed the whole ordeal and gave me that 'be still' look that I knew so well. Nodding at him, we both mouthed the word 'wait.'

The next morning amidst the seemingly never-ending rain, I headed to the garden to meet the Gardener. To my surprise, I found our camper's tent right in the middle of my greenhouse. Annoyed that he hadn't moved on, I let out a sigh, all the while trying to hide my frustration.

"Probably should get goin'..." Trav mumbled.

"Oh no! It's still raining! You can't go anywhere! Besides, I've prepared hot cinnamon rolls and a big pot of fresh coffee!" the Gardener interjected.

It smelled delicious, but I didn't want to share it with our intruder. I didn't know this guy from 'Adam' - who was he? For all I knew, he could be an escaped convict! Feeling a bit flustered, I sat down to join them.

"Good morning, Birdy! I've invited our new friend to join us for breakfast!"

"Ohhh... that's nice..." I responded, trying to have a good attitude.

The Gardener read my mind as usual. He gave me a big grin and handed me a cup of freshly brewed coffee. He then winked as if to say, 'Be still and wait.' I learned that if he was at peace, then I could be at peace as well. So, I dismissed my anxious thoughts and began to do what the Gardener did - simply love our new friend.

Weeks passed and each day seemed to be a repeat of itself. Both Trav and the rain became permanent squatters in the garden, and I began to wonder if either one would ever leave. As far as I could tell, he looked quite comfortable in his new location. And even though he said very little, he did manage to squeak out an occasional 'thank you' once in a while. It puzzled me though. Why did he land in *my* garden? Did he ever plan to move on and what was I supposed to do with him? Yet with every question that filled my mind, the Gardener's calm but firm look simply said, 'Wait!'

I began to understand the meaning of waiting *patiently* as the gray cloudy days stained my face with the rain's own teardrops. When I say *patiently*, I mean I learned how to accept and tolerate delays, problems, and suffering without becoming annoyed or anxious. It meant that I needed to love no matter how inconvenient it appeared.

April finished the same as it began, and May rolled in toting more gray clouds and drizzling rain. Although now, for some reason, the unrelenting weather no longer bothered me. A change occurred inside as I learned to become a good 'waiter.' To wait on the Gardener meant to rest in his good plans alone, no matter what the outward circumstances dictated. Yes, I could wait well, knowing I wouldn't be disappointed. So, I patiently waited and dodged the downpour, while I tried to make our company feel as comfortable as possible.

"There is so much to be thankful for!" I declared one morning as I glanced through my rain-splattered window towards the garden. "I want to do something extra-special for the Gardener and Trav today. I know... I'll throw big festive garden party and celebrate life with my friends!"

I quickly put on my apron and got to work making the Gardener's favorite meal - fried chicken, potato salad, a garden salad, and an apple pie. After arranging it neatly in my basket, I headed to the greenhouse.

"Good morning!" the Gardener welcomed, even though it was almost noon when I arrived.

He seemed delighted to see me, especially with my basket of food.

The Gardener promptly laid out his plaid blanket on the floor, unpacked our lunch and arranged the banquet before our guest.

"Wow!" Trav exclaimed.

His eyes grew as big as saucers and he gave me a thankful nod before heartily digging in. Meanwhile, the Gardener and I chatted over our meal. Our seemingly permanent visitor sat in his usual silence and devoured his food. Yet I could tell by his demeanor that he heard every word we spoke.

"So tell us why your parents call you Trav... is it a family name?" I politely asked, wanting to include him into our conversation.

"Oh, that's my nickname... I'm a Traveler looking for land that I can spend my life making into a garden... just like this one. But I'll probably end up traveling the rest of my life 'cuz I don't deserve a garden."

He paused to look down and shook his head as if he wanted to escape a world of dark memories. Meanwhile the Gardener and I quietly listened.

"I once had a plot of grassy land when I was a kid. We played football and other games on it. I loved that land. But I pretty much destroyed the whole thing when I got older. I abused it trying to get some kind of pleasure and satisfaction. Yeah... I used it for a lot of bad things 'cuz I wanted everyone's approval... that failed though! My friends and I trashed it until it got ruined... so we abandoned it. But I don't want to talk about it. All's I know is the property got infested with every vile memory... I hated the land. That's when I decided to start a new chapter and become a good person. Now I'm searching for a new field. I could never go back to that old place and I don't think it's fixable. It certainly couldn't look like this garden. Besides... even though I said I owned it, the land didn't belong to me. I don't know who owned it. I don't think I could ever forgive myself for what I did to it!" Filled with shame and remorse, he continued, "I definitely don't deserve a garden... but my dream is to have one like yours... although I don't know how to get one... and couldn't afford it anyway. Yeah, I'll probably just wander 'til I die. I suppose the name 'Traveler' fits me and... that's pretty much the story of my life..."

Surprised and shocked by our Traveler's tale, I looked at the Gardener with amazement. He said more in the last few minutes than he'd communicated all month. Everything made sense to me now. He wasn't just Trav - he was a Traveler searching for his own garden.

"Oh my!" I quietly mouthed as I processed all this new information.

Everything in me wanted to blurt out my own story. I glanced at the Gardener and waited for his approval. He immediately grinned and gave me a nod that said, 'It's time! Go for it!' I felt like a racehorse let out of the gate. With the Gardener's full blessing and authority, I confidently began.

"Can I tell you my story?"

"Sure... if you want..."

"Well, here we go then... this land began as a nasty plot of soil just like yours! But the Gardener never designed it this way. He destined every 'hume-man' to have a garden that looks just like his. 'Hume' is another word for soil, which is where all 'hume-man' life came from. This is why every 'hume-man' seeks a garden of life... otherwise, their soil will remain lifeless and barren."

"Yeah... that sounds like my plot. It's pretty hopeless!"

"Oh, but that's not the end of my story! The Gardener purchased a plot of earth for each one of us. But the problem is, most people don't know about it or even want it. So, it lays derelict, trafficked and left for ruin... by our enemy."

"Enemy?" Traveler questioned, still trying to understand.

"Yes, we all have an enemy. He calls himself the Inspector. He goes around telling everyone they're not worthy of having a garden. When we finally receive our gardens, he thinks it's his job to tell us how bad they are. He is a liar and his agenda is to destroy all gardens."

"Why would he want to do that?" our Traveler inquired, scratching his head.

"He hates flourishing gardens because they reflect the Gardener's beauty, and he hates the Gardener above all. That's why he tried to put a big *Rejected, Condemned, and Uninhabitable* sticker across all 'hume-manity' hoping to keep us blinded by his lies. You see... each person yearns for their own garden. Have you ever noticed how everyone is searching for a paradise of life that will identify them? It's because the Gardener created us with an inner need to inhabit the garden he intended for us. You could almost call it a spiritual memory that we crave. Yet, in our finite thinking, we don't fully understand why the desire is there. Truth is... everyone needs a Gardener! Without the Gardener, there can be no garden... no resurrection or beautiful life. Apart from his work, every one of us has a barren destiny of doom. He alone has the perfect blueprint... no one else has the knowledge, skill, supply or strength to create your garden into its intended destiny... of glory."

"Glory?"

Trav gave me a blank look like he didn't have a clue what I meant.

"When I say *glory*, I mean the beautiful manifestation of the Gardener's loving character. He wants to fill our gardens with *his* wonder and *his* life! No one else can do this... but him!"

Every time I told my story, I passionately bubbled with excitement. I knew this truth contained the power to transform people's lives. And oh, how I wanted Trav to hear and see the truth for himself!

When I finished, I could tell he didn't know what to do with everything I shared with him. He looked puzzled, stunned, overwhelmed, amazed, and thrilled all at the same time.

"I can't possibly buy a garden like this one. I certainly can't afford a Gardener like the one you have!" he frowned, after calculating what he might bring to the table, which was nothing.

"My Gardener has already bought your property for you. It cost him everything he had, but he did it willingly because he loves you! He fully understands the worth of your garden and its created value. It doesn't matter what the land looks like now. The Gardener only sees what it will become once he restores it to its original destiny. It's *Good News!* And you don't have to hire him!"

"What do you mean?"

"I mean... he gardens freely... besides, no one can afford to pay him for all the work he does! But rest assured... since he's already bought your garden, you can trust him to nurture it and keep it as his own. He did it for me and he will do it for you! No one can do a better job... he alone does everything well!"

The Traveler sat in complete awe, hardly able to believe this could be true. I understood how he felt because I once felt the same way. It seemed too good to be true, yet every bit of it was true!

"Well... what do I need to do now?"

Not wanting to miss a single word of instruction, he took out a paper and pencil to write everything down.

"Let go of the past! Accept the Gardener's gift... he already paid for it... and now it awaits you!" I responded as he began to take notes.

"What exactly is that?" Trav asked, trying to comprehend all I said as if his life depended on it.

I paused for a second to carefully choose my words, "You must understand the Gardener has not only given you a new garden... but above all, he wants to be *your* Gardener! Get to know him. Simply receive his love and personally invite him to come and cultivate your land... then let him set to work. Oh, and also take lots of time to read the title deed to your land... become well-acquainted with it. You need to believe everything it says so you can take hold of what is yours and make the most of it. If you don't understand what belongs to you, the enemy will try to steal it. When you know what is yours, you can begin to live from *this* place of truth. As the Gardener plants your garden... don't be afraid to say 'yes' to all that he desires to do. You must recognize that his work is always for your best! Your greatest joy will be waking up every day to meet him in your garden. Whatever you do, don't try to garden by yourself. Simply 'do life' with the Gardener. Enjoy him and trust all of his decisions. Let his love become your safe place. I guess you could say that you just need to live every moment in constant relationship with him. Learn to hear and trust his gentle whispers, and don't be afraid to respond to all he says. This will make your garden flourish with life. But your greatest joy above all... is the Gardener will dwell in your garden and become your best friend. As you yield to his good plans, your garden will burst with new life! Now... I hope I haven't overwhelmed you with all this... don't worry! The Gardener will be there to gently lead you and nurture your garden until it becomes all

~ "Simply 'do life' with the Gardener.
Enjoy him and trust all of his decisions.
Let his love become your safe place." ~

that he intended it to be. He has to remind me of this all the time because I forget... but he is so patient! He is willing to wait as long as it takes to make your garden perfect."

The Traveler put away his pencil and paper and sat quietly as if he safely arrived to shore after being shipwrecked at sea.

"Look! The rain has stopped... can you believe it?" I announced with a big grin.

The clouds disappeared, and the sun already set to work drying the waterlogged soil.

"I suppose... this means it's time for me to fulfill my destiny!" Trav declared.

Overwhelmed and anticipating the garden that awaited him, our precious Traveler eagerly packed up his few belongings. With his backpack on and ready to go, he gave me a big hug.

"Thanks for putting up with me for the last few months... you taught me how to hope again."

"I'm going to miss you, Trav!" I said, feeling a lump in my throat.

"Yeah... me too!" his voice quivered.

Then he turned to the Gardener, and they embraced like a father and son who longingly missed years apart but were finally reunited to live forever. Without warning the dam that held my tears of joy broke open into floods.

All at once, I felt the warm sun on my back as its rays streamed through the greenhouse windows, heating up the entire shelter.

"Let's go enjoy the sun!" I said, wiping my eyes.

As we stepped outside, the garden greeted us with kisses of pink and white blossoms. Meanwhile, the newly-budding leaves on the trees opened their tiny faces towards the sky. Every flower miraculously unfolded into full bloom in what seemed like only minutes. Even the tulips and daffodils awakened from their winter nap and poked their heads out of the ground. The entire garden glistened with light as new life announced its grand entrance into spring.

"Anything else I need to know?" our Traveler asked, turning to give me one last hug.

"Don't ever be afraid to wait on the Gardener's plans! You can always trust him! Always, always!" I answered, speaking from experience.

"You're right! The best thing that I've ever done is waiting with you and the Gardener these past months. Thank you again! I could never repay you!"

"It's all paid for!" the Gardener beamed.

"Please come back anytime," I invited, opening the gate as our guest left the garden.

"I will!" he promised, turning to wave goodbye.

We both waved back as he walked down the street and disappeared around the corner.

"I'm going to miss that guy!"

"*Waiting* changes everything, doesn't it Birdy?" the Gardener replied, inspecting the little blossoms popping out all over the cherry tree.

Feeling relieved that spring finally arrived, I let out a happy sigh, "You're right! I guess it's time to move forward! What a welcome sight this sunshine is!"

"It is indeed!"

"Are we going to plant any new seeds?"

"I already did! I planted them in March, and they got watered the whole month of April and May. See the little sprouts already peeping through the ground? Now, all we have to do is wait!" he said with a big smile and a twinkle in his eye.

Of course, everything made sense to me now. The Gardener planted his 'seeds' of love in our new friend. We watered them for the last couple of months, nurturing them daily in our greenhouse.

Today we saw new life spring out of the ground.

"You could say we sowed in tears, but today we reaped in joy!" I declared, squeezing his hand.

"Yes, my dear Birdy, a new garden was birthed today!"

"You have not only taught me how to wait *patiently* on you, my dear Gardener... but you have also taught me... you will never disappoint when I do!"

CHAPTER 16

Seeds Of Grace

"Birdy... Birdy... Birdy... Birdy!" called the sweet tweeting that awakened me this morning.

"Who's that chirping my name?" I said through a yawn as I sat up in bed.

I looked out the window and saw a beautiful red cardinal perched on my windowsill.

"Well, good morning to you too!"

"Birdy... Birdy!"

"Okay... give me just a minute to get ready!"

I quickly dressed and headed out to the garden with my new feathered friend flying above me.

"Top of the morning to you!" the Gardener greeted with a tip of his cap and a smile.

"And to you as well! It looks like it's going to be a great day!" I cheerfully chimed.

"Yes, it is... and great plans await you my dear!" he agreed, motioning for me to join him on the grass. "Look what I have for you!"

He showed me his thermos of freshly brewed coffee, a basket of his famous cinnamon rolls, and a brown burlap bag.

"Yay! My day just got even better! So... what are you carrying in that sack?"

"You'll have to wait and see... but before I show you, tell me why you think today is going to be such a great day!"

"Well, first of all, the cinnamon rolls and coffee are amazing as usual. Secondly, it's a perfect summer day... the garden is in full bloom and everything looks absolutely delicious. And thirdly, something good always happens when I'm with you! Need I say more? Life is just wonderful!"

"You're right! Life is wonderful! Don't ever be afraid to dream big and expect more. This whole garden is made with *more* than what you see!" the Gardener grinned with an extra twinkle in his eye. "Would you like to go over today's plans?"

"Sure, I'd love to!"

He laid the burlap sack on the ground in front of me and grinned.

"Are you going to tell me what's in there, or do you want me to look for myself?" I giggled in my usual, nosey way.

"This, my dear, is what we are going to do today."

Then opening the satchel, he handed me a packet of seeds.

"What exactly are these?"

"They're seeds that I harvested from every single plant in this garden. I've collected them over the seasons so we could share them with all our visitors."

"Great idea..." I said, dumping the whole sack out on the ground, "but don't you think it would be nice to have pictures on the front so people can see what they will grow into?"

"Well, I've written the names of each plant and flower on the packets. If people ask what the seeds will become, you can show them the actual plants right here in our garden!"

The Gardener took the bag and cleaned up the mess I made.

"I don't want to infringe on your plans, but... can I help give them away?"

"Of course you can! These seeds are from your garden and you should be the one to hand them out. If you need any questions answered, I'll be nearby."

I gave him a nod, picked up the burlap bag, and flung it over my shoulder.

"Look, Birdy! There's already a line of people outside the garden. Let's see who's come to visit us... on this 'perfect summer day'! Would you mind opening the gate?"

"At your service! Whatever you bid Master Gardener!"

Even though our special time together seemed shorter than usual,

I didn't question his eagerness to get on with the morning. I knew he continuously worked outside the box and I learned to welcome his spontaneity, which always kept my life very interesting and truly miraculous.

As I welcomed our guests, I felt heaven's skies smile upon me. Like a bunch of little birds, they chattered about in anticipation. That is, except for a scruffy, gray-haired man in worn-out blue jeans and a brown corduroy jacket with ripped leather patches on the elbows. His eyes looked sad and weary. The rest of his face remained hidden underneath his thick gray beard and an old straw hat. He appeared timid and almost embarrassed to be there, so I went out of my way to be friendly.

"Come on in and enjoy the garden! You're welcome to pick any fruit or flowers, and feel free to drink from the fountain if you like. It's right in the middle of the garden," I offered.

He put his hands in his pockets in hopes of finding some form of payment.

"Well, I haven't any money, so can I just browse?"

"Oh, there is no cost sir, this garden has been freely given to me. Please help yourself!"

Before he could answer, I politely excused myself and set out to deliver the packets of seeds like party favors.

"Here, would you like a packet of seeds?" I asked a little red-headed lass.

"Can I grow these in my own garden?"

"You sure can!" I grinned.

"Yay!" she squealed.

"May I have a few extra packets for my friends?" her mom asked.

"Of course... we'll never run out!"

I quickly offered her several more, just to see her face light up.

"How and when should I plant these?" a young man inquired.

"There's the man you need to talk to... he can help you with anything you need to know!"

I pointed to the Gardener who stood by ready to answer his questions.

Everyone hungered for love, and even the smallest act of kindness meant so much to them. Finally, after I gave each person a packet, I returned the burlap bag to the Gardener.

"You forgot the gentleman sitting over in the bird sanctuary," he gently prompted.

"Thanks... who did I miss?"

I headed over to find out who I forgot, only to discover the older gentleman in the brown corduroy jacket sitting in an Adirondack chair. Who was he? He looked haggard and battered by life.

"Hello sir, would you like some seeds? You can plant them in your garden."

The man looked at the packets and despondently replied, "They're no good to me. Might as well be a bag of stones."

"What do you mean they 'might as well be a bag of stones'?"

"I don't have a garden," he mumbled as he stared at his feet.

"Well, would you like a garden?" I asked, attempting to cheer him up.

"Oh no... I could never have one! I destroy everything I touch!" he whimpered.

"Sir, you may not be able to grow a garden by yourself, but I know someone who delights in creating gardens!"

"Who's that?"

"He's my Gardener. You see, these seeds appear to be useless stones to someone who doesn't realize the life inside them. The Gardener takes these seemingly dead pebbles and breathes life into them... they'll become beautiful flowers when you plant them in your garden! Do you like these?" I asked, pointing to the bluebells and yellow buttercups around us.

"Y... y... yes... th... they... are very nice," the older man stammered as his eyes scanned the garden.

"Do you know... everything you see here came from these tiny seeds. They can turn a desert into a flourishing wonderland! You wouldn't believe the state of my garden before the Gardener came to live in it. I completely destroyed it... it looked like nothing more than a disgusting plot of useless dirt! Well, at least that's what I thought!"

I wanted to sow a seed of hope into his desolate thoughts. Oh, how I prayed he would see that he too had a Gardener who desired to give him a garden like mine.

"You don't know what I've done!" he mumbled.

"It can all be forgiven, sir... every last bit! That's what the Gardener does!"

The old man stared at the grass as tears rolled down his face. What was I supposed to do with this perfect stranger bawling like a two-year-old? I felt so helpless.

"Would you like to meet the Gardener?" I asked, hoping he would say 'yes.'

"Wh... why? I don't think anyone can help me at this point," he answered as he wiped his tears on the back of his sleeves. "But... could I have a packet of those seeds? They'll remind me of how beautiful your garden is, and well... they're probably the closest I'll ever get to owning a garden myself," he said with a feeble laugh.

Just then the Gardener came over and began to talk with him, "Tell me your story."

"Well... I'm an alcoholic. Been that way for years. I lost everything... everything... my job, my family, just... everything. I walked out on my family years ago," he sorrowfully recalled.

"Why did you do that?" the Gardener tenderly inquired.

"'Cuz I hated who I was and what I did to them!" his lips quivered, fighting back the tears.

"What did you do to them?" the Gardener asked.

"I'd go into drunken rages and beat my wife and kid... practically every day... that's all I knew to do. My Paw always beat me, and I suppose I'm just like him. I haven't seen my family in years. Could never forgive myself," he recounted in bitter remorse.

He put his hands over his face and began to sob again. I looked at the Gardener, unsure what to do while our visitor attempted to regain his composure.

"Why don't you tell this gentleman about your life?" the Gardener turned and asked.

Without any hesitation, I nodded and began to share my story, "Well, my father was an alcoholic too..."

I didn't know why I started with that information, but that's just what came out.

"My dad beat my mother and me... when he got drunk. One day he left the house and never came back. Years passed and my mother died leaving me to fend for myself. Honestly, I made a mess of my life. But the day came when I discovered the Gardener bought me a garden. I simply needed to accept his invitation and allow him to transform my plot into a garden. I brought nothing to the table except a glimmer of hope... that maybe... my life could be more than dirt. The Gardener took my tiny seed of hope, removed all of the wreckage and then planted his own seeds of life into this once-desolate property. His seeds looked no bigger than the ones I gave you, but once he planted them, a whole new garden of life awaited me. When I remember why I destroyed my plot of land, I could understand why my father drowned himself in the bottle..."

"Why's that?" the old man shot back.

"...because he believed the same lie that I did," I answered, shaking my head.

"What lie?"

"He believed he would never amount to anything... but dirt... and that lie drove him to escape his own life. He didn't understand that he too could be *more than dirt!* Ohhh, what I would give to tell him that truth now!"

As I looked into the old man's eyes, my heart flooded with overwhelming compassion. I hoped my words would shed a sliver of light into his life.

"You don't understand... people like us don't deserve anything!" the man replied in disbelief. "You were hurt by your father. How could you ever forgive him? I would never expect my family to forgive me... ever!" he said, bursting back into tears.

I handed him a tissue and answered, "But I do forgive him! I forgave him long ago! When I understood the Gardener's destiny for me, I saw my dad's destiny as well... and my heart broke for him. How I wish I could see him again and help him understand the truth of how precious he is to the Gardener... if he's still alive... but that would be a miracle."

~ *"He believed he would never amount to anything... but dirt... and that lie drove him to escape his own life. He didn't understand that he too could be more than dirt!"* ~

On the verge of tears myself, I mustered up the best smile I could.

"Well, there's no garden for an old Ganel like me! I wish there were, but how could I ever forgive myself?"

As he hung his head in despair, his straw hat fell to the ground exposing the last little bit of hair combed over his balding scalp.

"What do you mean 'old Ganel'?" I asked.

"Oh, that's what everyone calls me. My real name is Eden Ganel."

Just then the Gardener interjected, "I know someone else with that same last name." Then looking at me he said, "Why don't you tell this man your name?"

I stood in silent shock. My mind scrambled to sort through all the facts. This guy had the same name as my dad! Could it really be him? I stared at the ground while I frantically searched for an explanation as to who this man might be. Is this what my dad looks like now? I hadn't seen him in years and couldn't identify him under his bushy beard. He'd only remember me as a child and wouldn't recognize me now. How did he get into my garden anyway? What if it was him?

'Could... this be... my dad?' I wondered as my whole body trembled.

My heart pounded at the realization that this could be *my dad* right in front me. Daring to look into his eyes, I knew they were, in fact, the same eyes of the man in my memories. But now, I saw no anger behind them, only brokenness and pain.

Still stunned, I swallowed hard, "My name is Grace Liberty Ganel... but my mom used to call me Birdy."

"Oh no!" the old man cried, putting his hand over his mouth in disbelief.

Forlorn, yet suddenly hopeful, he jumped to his feet and reached towards me in the most vulnerable way he knew.

"Gracie, my dear Gracie... how can you ever forgive me?" he sobbed. "Look at you, just look at you! What a beautiful garden you have! Your life is so complete... considering all I did to wreck it. Oh... for... forgive me... my dear Gracie... will you please forgive me... please?" he begged through tears of remorse.

"I already have Daddy... I did a long time ago!"

Tears of joy rolled down my cheeks as I ran into his arms. Freely I could love. How wonderful to set others free.

"Daddy, I was never dirt... and neither are you! You have a wonderful garden that awaits you and the best Gardener one could ever imagine. Please give him a chance!" I pleaded.

The old man nodded 'yes' and then kissed my forehead over and over, saying, "Thank you, thank you... thank you, my dear Gracie!"

I took hold of my dad's hand and reached for the Gardener with my other hand. The three of us embraced in complete restoration.

"Dad... do you know what 'Grace' means?"

"Not really..."

"It means 'undeserved, unmerited favor.' This is what's been given to you and me. Do you know what 'Liberty' means? It means we're free to live and love and not look back. Do you know what 'Ganel' means?" Before he could respond, I continued, "It means 'Garden of God!' When you named me, you didn't even realize my name meant 'undeserved favor, free and full of life... a Garden of God'... that's who I am! I am loved and so are you! You are a 'Ganel' too! It means that you're a 'Garden of God' as well!"

The Gardener joyfully chimed in, "Did you know that 'Eden' means... a delightful garden?"

"I'm not a delightful garden! How could there be anything delightful about me? Remember that horrible storm... the one when we got stuck in the gazebo? Well, I thought neither of you would ever want anything else to do with me after how I acted that day. Can you forgive me for my nasty attitude? I'm so sorry for what I have done... I'm so wretched!"

The Gardener winked at me as if to say, 'I told you he'd be back!'

"That was you?" I blurted out, now almost laughing. "You're the grumpy old man that threatened to sue us?"

~Freely I could love.
How wonderful to set others free. ~

"Yeah, that's me, but... but... you... you... were so kind... and happy... and sooo peaceful throughout the whole storm... even when everyone else was so horrible to you!"

"That's all in the past," I replied with a smile.

"Well, I never forgot it! Your kindness made me want to return... but I couldn't muster up the courage until today. I hoped you wouldn't recognize me. My beard is longer now and well, I suppose my hat does hide my face a bit. Will you forgive me? I had no idea that it was my own flesh and blood singing with such an angelic voice. Your song is what caused my heart to hope again..."

Completely choked up, I cried out, "Daddy... I forgave you then... even when I didn't know it was you! And I assure you I haven't thought about it since. You are forgiven... and the past no longer needs to be lamented over... or feared in any way."

I reached out and gave him a great big hug, although I don't think he knew what to do. But he welcomed it in his own awkward way.

"The Gardener already gave his all to buy you a garden. You have a destiny beyond your own performance... or ability... you must understand that he sees you according to what he created you to become. It's time to let go of the past... and embrace the Gardener's gift... it patiently awaits you. From now on, you must only live from what the Gardener has done and will do for you!"

I didn't know if he fully understood everything I said, but I knew he would in time.

"Could there be a new chapter for me as well?"

He paused a moment, revealing his inward battle to hope again.

"I... I..." his lips quivered while he wiped his tears. "I... hope I'm not *too* old or *too* ruined, or... or *too* late to have a garden like this. It seems *too* good to be true."

"No, you are never *too* old or *too* ruined, or *too* late... Mr. Eden Ganel!" the Gardener promised with a smile, patting his back affirmatively. "Remember, my grace or 'unmerited kindness' is your empowerment to attain all I have purposed for you."

"I want you to be my Gardener... will you take my ruined field? I want nothing to do with it... will you make me a garden?"

"That's what I do! I remove the old and replace it with a brand-new garden of life... for all eternity."

"Thank you, thank you... I'm forever indebted!"

They embraced for several moments. None of us said a word until my dad looked up with a big, peaceful grin.

"I'm ready to begin anew... and... I don't have to do this by myself... do I?"

"Oh no, I'll be there... and will never leave you!" the Gardener promised.

"Dad, your part is to get to know the Gardener... receive all he has given you... love him with everything in you... and waste no time doing whatever he asks you to do... he'll do the rest."

"How can I not love him... he purchased my garden for me. I can't imagine what it will look like... but I hope it's similar to this one!"

"One thing I can assure you of... he will not let you down... look what he's done with my garden. Would you like me to give you a tour?" I asked, hoping to inspire him with new vision of what the Gardener desired to do for him as well. "We still have a little time before the sun sets."

"Yes, yes! I would like that very much!" he quickly responded, his head nodding up and down.

We spent the rest of the day catching up. As I guided him around the garden I showed him what each seed would look like once it reached full maturity. With every vibrant bloom he saw, he became even more excited about his own garden.

"I didn't realize the value of these seeds until I saw their blossoms in your garden. Can I have all of them in my garden as well?"

"Of course, you can... that's what the Gardener does!" I grinned from ear to ear.

"Yes, I make gardens beautiful in their perfect time... and yours has a wonderful destiny as well!" the Gardener assured.

"I guess this is *my* time, isn't it?"

"Indeed, it is!"

By now, the sun bowed its head below the horizon, and the visitors began to meander home.

"I suppose it's time for me to leave as well. I need to get some rest because I have a very important engagement tomorrow... I'm meeting with *my* Gardener!" our new Mr. Eden Ganel announced.

His eyes twinkled, and he let out a little laugh. Then he turned and gave each of us a big hug goodbye.

"Dad, promise you will come and visit soon!"

"Yes... yes, I will!"

"I look forward to our next visit!" I said as I kissed him on the cheek.

He looked startled and pleased at the same time.

"I struck your precious face all those years ago, but today you have honored me... kissed my face... and given me new life! Thank you, my dear Gracie... thank you!"

I love you, Daddy!"

I could tell he knew it. He squeezed my hand and tenderly smiled before hurrying out of the garden. For the first time in his life, a hope and a future awaited him. Delighted and stunned, I watched him walk down the street until he disappeared out of sight. The Gardener and I looked at one another.

"Wow! I never imagined... I would *ever* meet my dad again. What an amazing day!"

I let out a contented sigh and wiped my remaining tears of joy.

"Yes, it's been a miraculous day indeed!"

"My dad's alive! He celebrated his first day of life today! Did you know he would be here?" I asked as I closed the gate, still trying to put the puzzle pieces together.

The Gardener gave me a warm smile and his eyes beamed with satisfaction. Everything went according to his perfect plans.

After pausing a moment, he gently said, "Sometimes we only see dead seeds, but it's miraculous what happens after we plant them. The result is a beautiful life... a wonderful life... and a very fruitful life! Well done, Grace Liberty Ganel! I'm so proud of you! Today you reaped a beautiful harvest from the seeds of grace you planted on that stormy day... years ago."

"I had no idea what my simple kindness would turn into... but those seeds were born from the fruit of grace that *you* planted in my own heart long ago!"

"That's what grace does. It bears fruit that continually yields more and more fruit. Seeds of grace, my dear! Seeds of grace!"

The day's events left a joyful peace hovering over the whole garden.

"I wonder what time it is?"

I let out a big yawn as we watched the moon tiptoe into the night sky.

"It looks like we have a tired Birdy."

"I am tired, but a very happy tired... it's been one of the best days of my life!"

"Well, I think it's time to put your best day to rest... the sun has already gone to bed, and he beckons you to join him."

I leaned on the Gardener's shoulder and he christened my head with a sweet kiss.

"Sweet slumber, Birdy!" he softly whispered.

"Goodnight, my dear Gardener!"

"Goodnight!"

~ *"Sometimes we only see dead seeds, but it's miraculous what happens after we plant them."* ~

CHAPTER 17

Sundays

The Gardener's eyes twinkled with excitement as I entered the garden this morning.

"Happy Sunday to you, Birdy!" he greeted with a smile and a bright golden sunflower.

"And happy Sunday to you too! I love sunflowers... this one is especially beautiful... I think I'll leave it right here in this vase to welcome all our guests."

"Good idea, my dear!"

"Are you ready for this day?"

"Absolutely! Sundays hold a special place in my heart."

"Is it your favorite day of the week?"

"Well... they're all my favorite... but it's always good to rest from my labors and simply enjoy my handiwork. How would you like to go for a walk with me? I want to show you the ancient paths that I found buried for generations."

"Sounds great... I'd love to see them!"

The Gardener squeezed my hand and we set out for a Sunday stroll. As we meandered through the beautiful garden, he stopped at an old cobblestone path.

"This is thousands of years old, but notice... it's still as usable today as when I first laid it."

"Wait... you laid these stones?"

"Yes, every single one... and there are many more of these paths in the garden. Each time you find one, remember it will lead you to where you need to be."

"Wow! I didn't know these were here... I can't wait to discover all

of them!"

We followed the cobblestone path and ended up at the fishpond.

"Let's sit here on the bench for a while and soak in the morning sun!" the Gardener suggested.

Absorbed in the restful moment, we watched guppies, goldfish, and pumpkinseed fish playfully dart around.

"It's so peaceful..."

Before I could say another word, he whispered, "Look... notice our tiny friend over there?"

He pointed to a slippery frog playing hopscotch on the lime green lily pads. The little fellow hopped around fully engaged in his frivolity until he noticed the Gardener out of the corner of his eye. Then, stopping his game, the frog faced him and began to croak as if he needed to deliver the most important message in the world.

"What do you suppose he's telling you? It's obvious he's

deliberately trying to communicate with you!"

"He certainly is... he's praising his Creator with all his being!"

Moments later, a songbird landed on the back of our bench and began to sing with everything in her. Shortly thereafter, a flock of doves appeared in the nearby mulberry tree and joined in. They cooed as if they rehearsed their part a thousand times over, and today they delivered their grand debut. Soon, every bird in the garden flew over to participate in the chorus of praise.

"Listen to all the birds worship!" I announced as they peeped, chirped, tweeted, cooed, and warbled in unison.

"Their voices blend in perfect harmony!"

Not wanting to miss out, the bunnies popped out of their holes and began joyfully dancing around us. Meanwhile, the squirrels dashed up and down the trees desiring to share in the celebration. Even a peacock displayed his array of ornamental feathers. I especially loved the pink flamingos leading the parade of thanksgiving. Before I knew it, the whole garden broke out in a symphony of united praise. Even the flowers opened their faces in full bloom while the trees clapped their hands. How could any part of his creation keep silent?

Undone and bursting with gratitude, I couldn't help but join in. A new song flowed effortlessly from my lips as the entire melody unfolded into a beautiful anthem of adoration. With my hands lifted and my heart filled with awe, I worshipped my garden's Creator and Savior.

> *You love me, and You've made me Your own!*
> *You have purchased a ruined dirt field*
> *And turned it into a Royal Garden!*
> *To reflect Your image! You are my life!*
> *And I'm a reflection of Your goodness!*
> *A reflection of Your goodness!*
> *A reflection of Your goodness!*

As I sang, I smiled at my reflection in the fishpond only to catch the Gardener's reflection smiling back at me.

You have given Your all, now I give You my all!
Your loving presence has transformed
This whole garden with life!
You are my life! You are my life!
And I'm a reflection of Your goodness!
A reflection of Your goodness!
A reflection of Your goodness!

The Gardener beamed like a father fully embraced by his daughter's affections. His love breathed life into my soul and now I couldn't help but respond with my whole being.

"Oh, if I could share your love with all who visit this garden... oh, that everyone would bask in your presence!"

"That's what I long for as well!" he agreed.

"Look at the sundial... can you believe it's already time to prepare for our Sunday garden tea party? Everyone loves them!"

"They do... they come from all over to participate!"

In no time at all, the Gardener and I made little chicken salad sandwiches, as well as cucumber and tuna sandwiches, each quartered and neatly stacked on a silver tray. Alongside stood a multi-tiered porcelain cake stand filled with freshly baked scones, all buttered and ready to be enjoyed. Of course, no scones would be complete without our homemade strawberry jam and clotted cream. Next to them sat several teapots of hot brewed tea, fresh milk, and our very own garden honey. In the center of the table for all to enjoy, I displayed the pièce de résistance - a large basket filled with newly-harvested, choice fruit from our garden. Finally, I placed a vase full of lovely red roses at the end of the table and stepped back to admire the beautiful banquet before us.

"What do you think? Isn't this..."

"...perfect! If you want my thoughts... I'd say that together we make a picture-perfect tea party..."

"...well, everything we do together is always perfect... and of course... it's your presence that makes everything truly perfect..."

"...and my presence shall never leave you, my dear," he smiled with delight. "Now, why don't you open the gate... and let the festivities begin."

Before long, the men assembled under the oak tree to discuss their gardens. Meanwhile, the women gathered around the picnic tables. The air buzzed with the sweet sounds of excitement and happy chatter. Their conversations were like apples of gold in settings of silver - delicious and life-giving.

I particularly enjoyed watching the children frolic about on the soft grass. After tiring themselves out, they gathered around the Gardener and listened as he recounted the story of my garden.

"Will you make me a garden someday?" asked a petite brown-haired girl, no older than five or six.

"Of course! I've already bought the land and started preparing the soil. Do you know that I'm very excited about your garden?"

"Why?" she asked in anticipation.

"Well, I've seen some daffodils starting to bloom there... and they are beautiful!" the Gardener assured, giving the little girl a big smile.

"Really? I'm excited too! Now I have my very own daffodils!"

The pint-sized girl clapped her hands with glee and quickly ran off to tell her mother the Good News.

"I'm making a special garden for each one of you!" he promised, reassuring the rest of the children.

"Oh, I would love to have a fountain in my garden!" said a hopeful red-headed, freckle-faced lass in pigtails.

"Can you put a bird sanctuary in mine... and lots of garden worms to feed them with?" grinned a toothless boy wearing glasses.

"I want a swing in mine, just like the one in this garden!" smiled a brown-eyed lad with curly black hair.

"Yes, yes, yes to all of your requests! It is my good pleasure to give you everything you see... and more! Now, I have a treasure to show you... right here in this garden. See that tree over where your mommies are sitting? Come with me! I want to show you what I found hidden in its branches."

The children eagerly followed him, anticipating the secret wonder that awaited them. He carefully separated the tree branches and gathered the little ones closer.

"Look! It's a robin's nest filled with bright blue speckled eggs!"

whispered the little boy with curly black hair.

Meanwhile, the rest of the children giggled with excitement. They loved these kinds of treasures.

"That's not the only surprise... I have one more to show you! Do you want to see it?"

"Yes!" they shrieked while jumping up and down.

"Will you help me check on our newest additions... born right here in this garden?" he asked with a twinkle in his eye.

The little ones enthusiastically followed him over to where our resident rabbit family lived. The bunnies knew the Gardener very well and trusted him completely, so they all came out to greet him. But as soon as the mama rabbit saw him, she quickly went back into her little dwelling.

"Why did she leave us?" questioned the pint-sized girl.

"You'll see... we need to wait quietly," he whispered, motioning for the children to sit down on the ground next to him.

Moments later, the mama rabbit appeared. One at a time, she carried out her three tiny newborn bunnies to show the Gardener. The children's eyes beamed as he let each of them hold the babies for a second or two. They smiled in absolute glee! The mama rabbit remained calm and peaceful throughout the whole ordeal. She seemed to welcome the chance to show off her new bunnies to his little guests. She knew full well the safest place for her young ones was in his complete care.

The Gardener played with the children for a while and then politely excused himself to go join the young adults by the fishpond. Without asking, he walked over and sat right in the middle of them, like one of their peers. They welcomed his company and immediately scooted over to make room for him. His older age made no difference; they still treated him like their best friend, and indeed he was! Regardless of their age, he possessed a unique ability to cultivate a relationship with each one. They all mattered to him and he took a special interest in every detail of their lives.

After investing in the teens, he then made his way over to the adults. By the end of the day, he visited with each person in the garden, not overlooking a single soul. His life-giving conversations left every heart filled to the brim with love. All the carefree chatter reminded me of a big family reunion.

Once everyone satisfied themselves with the banquet we'd prepared, the Gardener asked, "Birdy, would you be willing to take out your accordion and play a few songs?"

He knew I didn't like to play in front of people, but I would play my best for him. Besides, he never heard the notes I missed - only the heart notes I played. So, I pulled out my accordion and began to sing the Gardener's favorite melody. Before I knew it, a beautiful chorus arose from the eldest to the youngest. Everyone bubbled with joy and appreciation. As I glanced up, he gave me a wink that let me know he thoroughly enjoyed every second. We all did, so much so that I don't think anyone wanted the day to end.

The singing continued late into the afternoon until the sun began to set. After our last chorus, my precious friends packed up their belongings and thanked us for the lovely day.

"Goodbye, Emma! Goodbye, Mr. Brown! Goodbye, Miss Talula! Goodbye, Trav! Goodbye, Daddy! Goodbye children! Goodbye! Goodbye! Goodbye!" I called out.

With stirred up vision and a renewed hope, the joyful crowd waved back as they trickled out of the garden.

"What a wonderful day... did you enjoy it?"

I knew the Gardener relished every part of it, but I wanted to hear his response.

"Absolutely! My greatest pleasure is watching *my* creation rest in *my* goodness."

"I could tell... like a pebble in water, your pleasure rippled out to all who came today... especially me! This whole garden is undoubtedly your kiss of love... and today's celebration has been a feast for our souls."

Tired yet refreshed, we sat down on the swing to enjoy the last of the evening sunset.

"Look who's poked his head over the horizon!"

The Gardener pointed at the supermoon's face smiling at us.

"Where did the time go? I feel like a child at the end of Christmas Day not wanting it to be over."

I closed my eyes and took a deep breath, hoping to solidify every moment into my memory.

"It never has to stop... just keep walking on the ancient paths!"

"What exactly does that mean?" I asked, looking up at him.

"Today we walked on the ancient path of worship... let me explain... you are my beautiful workmanship... or painting... so to speak! Every piece of art bears its master's design and signature. Your garden carries my name because... I AM your Gardener. It's my name that determines the origin, identity, value, and life of this garden. The more famous the name is on a piece of artwork, the greater its worth. That signature alone defines the painting's true existence and value." Pausing to make sure I understood, he went on, "You will find your greatest pleasure and fulfillment when you lift up my name and show forth my work... it's your garden's true purpose... and where you are complete!"

"I think I understand... this garden is like a piece of art revealing its master's handiwork... when I manifest your name and shine your splendor... I will overflow with your glory! Is this what worship is?"

"Yes... this is the ancient path we followed this morning!"

"I want this precious truth to anchor and guard my life. Honestly... I... I couldn't imagine doing anything else. It would be a sorry existence to enjoy the many attributes of your goodness... yet not know you or be able to respond to you in full appreciation. I want to stay on this path... and continually walk in the same joy I felt today! Every good thing I have... you've given to me... but... what

~ *"You will find your greatest pleasure and fulfillment when you lift up my name and show forth my work... it's your garden's true purpose... and where you are complete!"* ~

can I give you in return?"

He didn't answer. Instead he nodded a 'keep going' smile, like a father watching his daughter tie her shoe for the first time.

"One thing I know for sure is... I can't out give your goodness. I didn't earn any part of your work, nor can I repay it. *You* are my exceedingly great reward! You alone... my dear Gardener, are worthy to receive my full adoration! The more I am able to comprehend your love for me, the more my soul ignites with thanksgiving and praise. To lift up the Master Artist's name is my greatest desire above all. Yes... it is perfectly right that I love you with everything in me. Honor and glory are the only responses I can give in return for your goodness! Of course... that's the answer... pure worship that will never stop for eternity!"

Without wasting another minute, I proclaimed my love for him with a big kiss on his cheek. I knew he'd created my garden for this very moment and it's where I thrived. The Gardener smiled at me with beaming eyes that only spoke of his utter delight. We both sat in reverent silence until I felt the warm touch of his hand reach for mine to help me to my feet.

"Birdy... the evening is drawing to a close," he bid ever-so-softly.

"I know... I wish I could stay here forever... I'm just not ready for it to end!" I lamented through a tired yawn.

"Me too... but for now, it's time to put this day to rest. There will come a time when I will take you home to my garden where the beautiful songs of worship will never cease." Then he gently kissed my forehead and whispered, "I will see you tomorrow, my love... may your sleep be sweet!"

"Goodnight, my dear Gardener!" I whispered.

~ *"Honor and glory are the only responses I can give in return for your goodness!"* ~

CHAPTER 18

Tell The World

Dark clouds loomed over every visitor entering the garden this morning. I recognized a few faces but didn't know most of them.

"Good morning! Welcome!" I greeted an impeccably dressed woman in a gray suit.

Without answering, she marched right past me pulling a small suitcase behind her. She looked a bit intimidating, but I didn't let that phase me. Instead, it gave me a greater incentive to reach out to her.

"Please feel free to drink from the fountain and help yourself to any fruit on the trees!" I cheerfully offered, hoping she would acknowledge my invitation.

"Thanks!" she responded, stopping to glance back.

She still didn't smile, but I could see her face begin to soften. Then she let out a big sigh and plopped down on a nearby bench as if she couldn't take one more step.

"Do you mind if I stop and rest here for a moment?" she asked, brushing the hair off her forehead.

Her flushed face looked weary and confused. She appeared to be a tourist or on some sort of trip.

"Oh, please feel free to relax and enjoy the garden! After all, that's what these benches are here for," I reassured her.

"I'm not from around here... and honestly, I feel a bit lost," she nervously confessed.

"Can I help you? I know the area pretty well."

"You are helping me... just by letting me rest in this peaceful paradise."

"Would you care if I sit next to you?"

"Go ahead... isn't this your garden?"

"Well, actually... I inherited it a long time ago."

Neither of us said a word for a while. I could tell she didn't want
to talk, so we quietly watched two purple and green hummingbirds
chase one another around the magnolia shrub. As they fluttered
about, I saw her face soften even more until she gave a little smile.

"Do you like the garden?" I asked, trying to make polite
conversation.

She let out a sigh of relief and answered, "It's... it's so full of life
here... yet there's nothing busy about it. Everything seems tranquil

200

and, in its place, as if... as if..."

She paused, struggling to find her words. Suddenly she burst into tears and put her face in her hands. Not sure what to do, I instinctively put my arm around her to comfort her.

"You're not here by chance... you're here because you are loved!"

However, I couldn't console her. Unable to suppress her torrent of tears, she got up and walked away. What should I do now? Her 'walls' were a mile high, and she evidently wouldn't allow any entrance into her well-guarded heart. She seemed like the type of person who needed to be in control and never lost her composure in front of people. So, I gave her plenty of space, hoping we could talk again before she left the garden.

Just then, a young man passed me with a devastated look on his face. He appeared stunned as if he'd just received terrible news. Dazed and numb to life, he stared right through me when I smiled at him. But before I could welcome him, two arguing voices interrupted my opportunity. Looking around, I saw a young father and mother with three little children and a newborn. They both wore tired faces marked by sleepless nights.

Overwhelmed by all the hopelessness before me, my heart flooded with compassion. What could I do to help ease the pain that I saw? How could I fix their broken worlds? How could I touch them with goodness?

The Gardener read my thoughts and whispered, "No dark cloud is allowed to affect this garden's atmosphere. Remember, the joy inside our paradise is much stronger than the outside oppression. You have the hope they need, Birdy."

He was right! I knew I needed to spread this joy to every person who visited. And today offered yet another divine occasion to love those I encountered. The Gardener desired a personal relationship with each individual. He loved them and wanted to give them their own garden of life just like mine. His passion had become my passion as well! How could I keep silent and not tell everyone about the precious life he intended for them? No, I couldn't let even one person go through life into a dark eternity without knowing him. I knew the answer and it burned like a fire within me! They needed to

~ "Remember, the joy inside our paradise is much stronger than the outside oppression. You have the hope they need, Birdy." ~

understand their true destiny.

"I desperately want to share the Good News. I must tell them what you've done for me and what you want to do for them... but how do I do it? How can I communicate it in a way that they can understand and receive for themselves?"

The Gardener motioned for me to follow him over to the garden wall.

"Here Birdy, have a seat for a moment," he instructed, pointing to an antique wooden park bench we found buried in the back of the garden.

As we both sat down, I began to think about our restored bench.

"Do you remember how rickety this was when we discovered it?" he asked.

"Yeah, I thought you would just toss it out or burn it. But you didn't! You're an expert at redeeming every piece of junk. You see a treasure in what everyone else considers trash. Look what you did with this old thing!"

"Well, I do love to transform the old into new! That gives me an idea... Birdy, why don't you stand on this bench and tell them about it?"

"About what?"

"About the bench!"

"This bench? Oh... of course! What a perfect idea!"

"I'll be nearby if you need me," he assured.

"You always are," I replied, giving him a big grin.

Then without a moment to lose, I stood on the bench and smiled as everyone walked by. I'll admit, I must have looked pretty silly. I felt weak and vulnerable perched up there while people stopped to stare. A battle raged inside me as voices in my mind tried to convince me that my plans would fail. But now I had to choose to whom I would listen. Would I listen to my fearful pounding heart? Or would I take a risk and trust the Gardener's good plans that he ordained for me to walk in? Constrained by love, I chose to obey his directives, knowing that his presence always attended my obedience.

I put myself out on a limb because he taught me that's where all the ripe fruit grows. Nope, no tree trunk hugging for me today! I could see ripe fruit that needed picking, and I was ready to go out on the limb and gather the harvest!

Curious as to why I stood on the bench, a group of children gathered around me. Before long, their parents joined them. The couple with the three kids and a newborn showed up as well. Both looked as if their argument still needed to be resolved. Others saw the crowd gathering and wandered over out of curiosity. Even the lady in the gray suit with the suitcase came and stood towards the back. She still appeared guarded and distant. The group continued to grow in size until every person in the garden gathered around the bench, each inquisitively staring at me.

"Where is the young man I saw earlier... the one who looked shocked?"

The Gardener said nothing, but his eyes directed me to his whereabouts. He stood right in front of me - how could I have missed him?

A great opportunity lay before me, and I would not let it pass by. Even if everyone thought I was strange, I needed to share the Good News! My heart overflowed with love! Surprisingly, no one left. They

~ Constrained by love, I chose to obey his directives, knowing that his presence always attended my obedience. ~

seemed to sense my love and patiently anticipated whatever came next. Not sure what to do, I looked at the Gardener. He gave me a wink and a confident grin, emboldening me with the authority I needed to carry on.

Then in full assurance, I stepped into faith's substance and began to share the revelation of my Gardener's love.

"I bet you are wondering why I'm standing on this bench right now... well, it's a long story, so I'll try to make it as short as possible. Will you please give me your attention for a few moments?"

I scanned the puzzled faces who wondered what this could be about. And to be honest, I surprised myself as well. The quiet introverted me would not have done this. Instead, an overwhelming love compelled me to share my story. I could only think about each hurting person before me. Thus, I began to tell the tale of the no-good, upside-down, throw-away bench and how the Gardener transformed it with his love.

"You see, even though this bench spent years buried in the ground... and should have been thrown away or burned... the Gardener saw more than what laid in the dirt!" I proclaimed enthusiastically.

The crowd drew closer, hungry to hear more of what I had to say. When I finished sharing the parable of the bench, I began to tell my garden's miraculous story. I spoke of how the Gardener knew all along that my abandoned plot was more than dirt. I explained how he bought it and restored it into the garden that everyone now knew and loved. As they listened, I could see that they too, desired to know him.

"The Gardener longs to meet you today... and he has something to give you!"

Every eye watched intently, and every ear waited to hear what he wanted to give them.

With a big smile, I continued, "He has not destined any of you to an eternal wilderness of destruction. Each of you has a garden that he bought for you... just like he bought mine! He desires to become your Gardener and transform your garden into the image of his own garden! You see, no one can have a garden without having a

Gardener. He alone has the ability and the perfect seeds needed to create it into a garden of life!"

I then invited him to come up to the bench so they could meet him. As he walked forward, the darkness in their eyes began to lighten with hope.

"Could this be true? Can we know the Gardener?" said the couple with the three children and a newborn.

"Would he really want to know me and give me a garden like this one?" the young man asked in wonder.

I marveled as each person met the Gardener for the first time. With every encounter, a beautiful transformation took place. It seemed like a big birthday celebration. Today they came to know him and fully appreciate what his love for them had cost. I witnessed the dark shadows that loomed over their faces vanish in his radiant light. Some cried tears of happiness, while others poured out their hearts to him.

I cannot tell you how excited I became when I saw the despairing young man talking with the Gardener. The burden he carried into the garden disappeared. He let out a sigh of relief that quickly turned into a great big happy smile. Choked up with emotion, I fought back my tears. The Good News he heard today erased the bad tidings that doomed him earlier. He spoke with the Gardener for several more minutes and thanked him profusely before they embraced. Before he left, he stopped and thanked me for taking the time to share my story with him.

"How are you doing?" I asked, eager to hear his answer.

"Amazing! You see... I came here completely devastated..."

"What happened?"

"It's a long story... when I was born, my birth mom couldn't take care of me... and I became a ward of the state. A few months ago, I discovered my parents' identity, and where they lived. When I contacted them last week, they wrote back and said they didn't want anything to do with me. I know all this must sound confusing."

"What about your adoptive parents?" I asked, trying not to be too nosey.

"When I was put up for adoption... no one ever chose me." He paused for a moment and then grinned from ear to ear, "But today I discovered the Gardener chose me before I was even born... and he's gone to great lengths to buy back my garden. Can you believe that I'm that valuable to him? My life is more than unwanted dirt... and I have an eternal destiny!"

A faraway look came over his face again, although this time he glowed in complete amazement.

"I needed a relationship with someone bigger than myself and today I found him! He's placed the sun back into the center of my world and now all my confusion is gone. The Good News is... I finally belong! I've never belonged to anyone in my life!"

"You do belong! Don't ever let any other voice in your life cause you to doubt it ever again!" I assured as I gave him a great big hug goodbye.

By now, the lady in the gray suit made her way up to the front of the crowd. The floodgates finally opened, and she talked a hundred miles an hour to the Gardener. She finally met the first person who truly cared about her. He tenderly looked into her eyes and carefully listened while offering an occasional nod. The realization that she now knew how much he loved her changed everything!

Not wanting to interrupt, I took a seat nearby and heard her explain that she was a flight attendant. Her airline gave her unexpected time off work, so she decided to come to town to surprise her boyfriend. But when she arrived, she found him with another woman. Her whole world had fallen apart. She felt she couldn't be worth much if he did that to her. But today she discovered a greater truth. Her real value came from knowing the Gardener gave his all to redeem her field of death into a paradise of his love. What started out as the worst day of her life became the best day! She finally understood her true purpose and value. Thus, began her transformation.

After our beautiful flight attendant finished meeting with the Gardener, she turned and walked over to me. Before I could say a word, we embraced and cried tears of joy.

"Thank you for introducing me to your Gardener!" she said as she wiped her eyes with the back of her hands.

206

"He's your Gardener as well!" I whispered.

"Yes, he is! I can hardly believe it... but I do believe it! I do! I love watching the precious relationship you have with him... it's like the two of you are one. I want that also! I can see that you and your garden are... well, you're his very favorite."

"Absolutely, I am his favorite... without a doubt! But so are you!"

"Well, I guess he doesn't have favorites, does he?"

"Actually... the Gardener has many favorites... all are equally precious to him. Do you know why I can say that?" Not waiting for her to answer, I continued, "Because our gardens all come with the same price tag. They cost him everything, and that is how much we are worth to him... absolutely everything! There is no greater gift a person can give you than their 'everything.' We are all his favorites and when I realize how favored I am, I begin to understand how favored you are!"

Tears of joy rolled down both of our faces again.

"Thank you! Thank you! Thank you... I don't want to go... but I should be on my way!"

"Please stay in touch and come back soon!"

"I will... I promise!"

I gave my new friend a great big hug and walked her to the gate. After a long hug, she left pulling her little suitcase behind her.

As the day came to a close, everyone bustled out of the garden filled with joy instead of gloom. I waved goodbye to the married couple with the newborn and three little children as they walked out together hand in hand. After we bid farewell to the last guest, I closed the gate.

~ *"We are all his favorites and when I realize how favored I am, I begin to understand how favored you are!"* ~

The whole garden celebrated the day's events. The birds sang their evening chorus while the animals scampered about. Even the leaves on the trees applauded in delight.

"What a wonderful day it's been! Your suggestion to tell the story of the bench was just what they needed to hear. Thank you so much... I love partnering with you!"

"Well... I think we make a great team!" the Gardener grinned, putting his arm around me.

Relieved and oh-so-happy, we sat in the gazebo and both let out a deep sigh of contentment.

"Do you realize we haven't stopped to eat all day long? But for some reason... I'm not hungry!"

"I understand! There's a deeper nourishment we gain from giving out... one much greater than food can give us."

"Yeah... it's really true... and it makes me hungry for more!"

"There's so much more that awaits us!"

The cool evening breeze blew over my sun-kissed face as I took the Gardener's hand in mine.

"I'm so full of joy and I don't ever want to lose it!"

"Birdy, you don't have to... remember... harvesting fruit is always a time of rejoicing! This is the joy set before us every single day!"

"*You* live in this joy all the time... don't you?"

"Yes, it's the same joy that spurred me to buy back your garden. It's the same joy that made even the piercings in my hands worthwhile. It's the same joy that makes me continually pour life into your garden and never look back. It's the same joy that made me invest my all for you."

"What joy was that?"

I already knew the answer, but I wanted to hear it again.

"That joy was you, my dear!" he winked, gently patting the top of my head.

No matter how many times I heard him tell me this, my heart still burst with gratitude.

"How wonderful to know I am loved... and to share that love with others is my true purpose! The reward of seeing others come to know you... is incomparable!"

The Gardener gave me a warm embrace while we sat silently enjoying the sweet atmosphere. Suddenly I realized how tired I felt from the day's activities. But it was a good kind of tired - as if I had run a marathon and won.

The sun now dipped far below the horizon, giving way for the moon to take its place in the evening sky.

"Do you see the bright Morning Star twinkling over there?" the Gardener asked, pointing towards the heavens. "He's inviting you to partake in another night of sleep."

"That sounds wonderful to me... I willingly accept his invitation."

I rubbed my sleepy eyes and let out a big yawn.

Then turning to look at the Gardener, I whispered, "Thank you for another lovely day!"

"You're welcome, Birdy! Thank you, too! We did this together!"

"That's what made it so special!"

With a smile, he squeezed my hand and softly bid, "Goodnight, *my joy!*"

"Goodnight!"

My joy, too, was complete.

CHAPTER 19

The Gardener's Garden

"Why am I so drained after a full night of sleep? Perhaps I'll perk up once I see the Gardener, he always makes me feel better."

I finished my bowl of oatmeal, put on my pale pink lamby sweater and moseyed out to the garden. My frail frame didn't feel the need to go anywhere in a hurry. So, I slowly strolled over to our secret place where I knew the early November sunshine would warm my body and rejuvenate my mind.

"How lovely to see you this morning, my precious Birdy!" announced the Gardener's cheerful voice. "Here, let me help you sit down on the swing."

Gently taking me by the hand, he steadied my arm while I settled myself next to him. Once again, I sat in the garden with my devoted Gardener by my side.

"Are you comfortable, Birdy?"

His tender tone soothed my weary mind and invigorated my soul.

"Yes, I am... I could sit here all day long."

The beautiful oneness we shared as I basked in his presence infused me with life.

"How are you feeling today?"

I sensed an extra softness in his voice as he spoke.

"My soul is at peace, but my body is just not ready for the day's work... honestly... I'd like nothing better than to stay right here with you in our secret place!"

"Well, I don't have anything scheduled... except to enjoy the day with you! How does that sound?"

I let out a contented sigh and smiled, "That sounds perfect to me!"

We quietly glided back and forth and listened to the robins chirp their morning songs. Soon my mind wandered down memory lane, and I began to reminisce about all the wonderful years we enjoyed together in the garden. But I couldn't keep my thoughts to myself and before long, I recounted every memory in full detail to the Gardener. He simply nodded and gave me a pleased grin that let me know I had his undivided attention.

"Many decades have gone by... and I have grown older and a bit more feeble in these last years."

"But you have grown in many other ways as well! Remember... my gardens never stop growing!"

"I suppose they don't... not as long as you're the Gardener... I don't need anything more, and I don't want anything less... just you. My only desire is to be with the one I love."

"Birdy, you know my favorite place is right here with you... and I've never left you... just like I promised."

"You are always with me... although, in the beginning... I didn't realize you were there... nor did I think I needed you beside me... but that's changed! Over the years, I've learned to continuously live in the awareness of your presence... to depend on your goodness above all else... and you have faithfully been there waiting to carry me through every second of my day. You're my 'constant'... more constant than the morning sunrise." I leaned against the Gardener's shoulder and continued, "You know, watching you has given me wisdom for everything in life. You've shown me what truly counts and what doesn't... what will last for eternity and what is only

~ "I don't need anything more,

and I don't want anything less...

just you." ~

temporal. Everything we do together is eternal. That's why I cherish your presence... above all else. Things that once mattered so much, don't matter at all these days. You've taught me only people, their gardens, and the words you wrote in my big brown leather folder will last forever."

"Do you remember when I asked you if you are living in what you believe or believing in what you live?"

"Yes... it took me a while to figure that question out, but I eventually understood. I think I am finally learning to live in what I believe."

"What's your secret key to doing this, Birdy?"

"The key is... always living with you as my Absolute."

"And what do you mean when you say, 'Absolute'?"

The Gardener's eyes twinkled. I knew he asked me these questions just so he could enjoy my answers.

"You are my Absolute... and that is why I cherish *you* more than life itself... and since you've become my Absolute, I have no regrets. It hasn't always been perfect or easy, but you are perfect! And your presence is where I find my hope and joy... even in the hardest times!"

"Hmm..." he stopped and rubbed his chin. "I do remember some of those tough times... but like they say, 'every cloud has a silver lining'!"

"They do... although, only in hindsight have I seen the pain-born benefits. Suffering through those winter blizzards has taught me I could fully trust and depend on your care... I remember how you would take my hand in those dark moments and gently whisper, 'Wait on me, this too shall pass... I have a plan!' Sometimes I would have to wait quite a while before I saw any answer. But no matter what happened, I learned to be at peace... even apart from the outcome."

"And what is the key to this peace?" he squeezed my hand, awaiting my answer.

"*You*... my perfect *Solution!* The scars on your hands and the title deed that cost everything... has settled this truth in my heart forever. They have shown me that I can trust your love no matter what... be

213

it good or bad weather! I have nothing to fear!"

"Yes, the storms do pass and eventually the sun comes out. Even the severest winters are swallowed up with springtime, and faithfully followed by summer's wonderful warmth."

"And... you constantly have a plan in place to turn everything evil into good... although it doesn't always end like I think it will!"

"What do you mean?"

"Well... it always turns out better than I can imagine!"

"Birdy, you know, no one plants a garden unless they have hope for tomorrow!"

"You're right... you always championed my destiny and I knew you would make everything beautiful in its time!"

We continued our journey over the past decades, discussing the many truths that knit our lives together.

"My, how rapidly the seasons have come and gone... almost as quickly as the days of the week," I recalled with a sigh.

"But none of it's been in vain! I designed each moment with a specific purpose to enable you to fulfill your destiny... and through it all... your outlook on life has changed."

"In what ways?"

"Your expectations have changed! You continually live in anticipation of my favor and my goodness!"

"Well, what more could I desire? Your favor and goodness have recalibrated my every thought... and enabled me to think like you, respond like you, and some say even talk like you... like we are one. Now my garden looks just like yours... your life has given me life!"

"Yes, sweet oneness is the essence of a perfect garden."

"I love this oneness... do you know that you're forever in my thoughts? On nights when I can't sleep, I take my well-worn leather folder from my nightstand and read over your comforting words. They're my wise counsel and constant companions. They reveal your heart and impart your wisdom for whatever I need at that moment. I've read your words over and over and spent many delightful hours meditating on your truths... each time I see more of you... and my soul is infused with life. Your words have become the very fiber of my being... and not one promise has failed me... because... you never fail."

"To fail you would be to fail myself... and that's not possible!"

Completely satisfied in his love, I sat silently and continued to ponder his faithfulness. He never once let me down. Even in the darkest hours, his love illumined me and taught me to expect life in every seed's death.

Our day seemed to pass by quickly. The Gardener rested his arm along the back of the swing and drew me near to himself, close enough to hear his heartbeat.

"Are you enjoying yourself?"

"Absolutely... every bit as much as you are!"

As I chattered on, he leaned in to hear every word, almost as if he were recording each detail in a special book.

"Birdy, what is your favorite memory in this garden?"

"Hmm... I've cherished them all! Everything from those active years when we worked long hours cultivating the garden, to the special times we spent here in the secret place on our swing. Oh... and how can I forget our picnics on your plaid blanket? All those tasty lunches you prepared for us... not a meal went by where we haven't gotten lost in one of our rich conversations. They were simply delicious..." Pausing to process my thoughts for a second, I looked up into his eyes, "Well, actually, what I treasure most of all... is being with you. You know, I don't have many passions these days, but I do jealously guard our time together. Your presence is what I live for... you are my best thought both day and night... I suppose that's why I've never missed a day in the garden with you."

"You know what I cherish most?" the Gardener asked as he stood up to stretch his legs.

"What's that?"

"You, Birdy! Our relationship has grown into a precious friendship... forever rooted and grounded in love!"

Then with a warm smile he extended his hand, "Would you like to take a little stroll with me? It won't be very far."

"Yes, I suppose I should get up and give my legs a bit of exercise."

The Gardener held out his arm and gently helped me to my feet. As we meandered through the orchard, I noticed its maturity.

"I'm amazed! My, how these trees have flourished. Notice the lush fruit still on their branches? It's your magnificent work from start to finish," I said, pointing to the trees bent over with ripe fruit.

"Would you mind if we stopped here for a second while I lift these sagging limbs? We need to undergird the pear tree before its bowing branches snap."

"Oh, look at this beautiful piece of fruit!" I exclaimed, noticing a big juicy pear dangling right before my eyes.

"Here, would you like it?"

Before I could answer, it literally fell off the tree into his hand.

"Why, yes! Thank you!"

I took a bite and its sweet juices burst all over my chin.

"Oh my, let me help you," the Gardener chuckled as he wiped my mouth with his handkerchief. "Do you know what tree this is?"

"Is this the old wild pear tree that you pruned almost to the ground all those years ago?"

"Those diseased branches had to die... this is the new tree that grew up in its place. It's a good tree, isn't it? Notice its abundant fruit... and see all the other trees around it? The seeds from this tree birthed every one of them."

"You certainly transformed it into a very good tree!"

"That's what I do... I make sweet... every bitter thing!"

"Your goodness is in everything you touch and everything you do! Honestly, I'm still overwhelmed with the realization that this garden was once just a pile of dirt... but of course, you saw *more* than dirt. Do you remember that first morning when you came to my house and gave me the title deed? You were quite persistent... like a man on a mission!"

The Gardener laughed, "I did have a mission... I saw much more! I saw this beautiful garden!"

As we headed back to our secret place, we passed my favorite rosebush decorated with the most fragrant roses one could ever imagine. After picking the most magnificent blossom, he carefully tucked its stem through the buttonhole of my sweater to be enjoyed the remainder of the day.

"Thank you! It's so beautiful!"

I buried my nose in its velvety petals for a moment and basked in its sweet fragrance.

"Do you remember when Verma came into my garden and stole all of my favorite flowers?" I suddenly recalled with a bit of a giggle.

"Yes, I do remember that day with Emma," he grinned.

"My, how she's changed over the years. You wouldn't even know she's the same person. She is the kindest, gentlest, most loving lady you could ever meet. Her garden is gorgeous, isn't it? I've never seen as much fruit on any tree as I've seen on hers. And she gives most of it away! To think, she just needed to be loved... whether I felt she deserved my love or not."

The Gardener simply smiled and gently assisted me back to the swing. After helping me get comfortable, he sat down and nestled me close to himself.

"Now what was I talking about... oh yes, Emma! How many people do you suppose have passed through this garden?"

"Many, many!"

"I stopped counting long ago when they ceased being just a number to me. You helped me to see every person the same way you see them. You taught me how to love every one of them."

"Each guest is a story of glory. Do you realize how many lives this garden has touched?" he beamed.

"It's the fruit of your labor. All your hard work has earned quite a reputation over the years. My family and friends characterize it with one word."

"And what word is that?"

"*Love!* It's undeniably your hallmark!" I affirmed while patting his arm in appreciation.

"Love is the source of all life and is the secret to why this garden flourishes."

"You certainly have lavished every inch of it with your love. Everyone can sense it the moment they walk through the gate!"

The Gardener took my hand in his as I continued talking.

"This garden has gone through so many chapters over the years, each filled with evidence of your miraculous life."

"Oh yes!" his face lit up as he pondered the years gone by. "My

~ *"Love! It's undeniably your hallmark!"* ~

dear Birdy, do you remember the early days when everything budded like an infant? Then we saw the years of rich growth with lots of healthy active development. Now in this last season, the garden rests in a sweet maturity. Did you notice that even though it produces more fruit now than ever before... there is a calm and serene peace that covers it?"

"That's because the garden has learned to rest in your presence... like a child nestled in her father's arms."

Just then, one of our resident rabbits hopped over to us. His little pink nose twitched as he jumped right into my lap.

"How precious... look at this little guy! This has never happened before... but it's just what I need today!"

The tiny creature snuggled into a ball as I stroked his soft brown fur. He seemed to relish every moment, although I'm not sure who enjoyed it more, the bunny or me.

We sat for quite a while until the sun began its journey downward. Could it already be this late in the afternoon? Mama rabbit knew the time because she called her little one home for dinner. Instantly my young friend gave me a nod as if to say, 'Thank you!' and scurried off to meet his mother.

As we quietly admired the sunset's golden hour, the Gardener tenderly looked at me and smiled. His timeless face never changed nor did his strength fail him for even a moment. He took my hand in his, still marked with the scars he endured for me. My hands looked so frail and wrinkly, but his remained strong and sturdy.

"Have you ever gotten tired of working in this garden?" I asked, realizing how much time and energy he invested over the years.

"Not for one single second!" he laughed.

"You still do as much around here as you did in the beginning... but most of your work is unseen!"

"What do you mean?"

"Well... you still dependably cut the grass, trim the hedges, water the flowers, and carefully tend to each plant with optimal care. Although... there is one thing you don't do as often anymore."

"What's that?"

"I haven't seen you pull weeds like you used to."

The Gardener nodded in agreement, "There aren't as many weeds as there were in the beginning. Now they slide out easily because their roots are not very deep, and it doesn't take long to remove them. The work I've done over the years is an eternal work that only flourishes with age... because gardens don't get old... they simply mature and bear more fruit!"

"This is true... this garden has matured beautifully... and every inch of it is the unprecedented work of your hands!"

"And I've loved every minute of it! On another note... are you hungry?"

The Gardener opened his rucksack and pulled out his freshly made sourdough bread along with a thermos of chicken noodle soup.

"I'm always hungry for your chicken noodle soup!" I eagerly responded, knowing that he used his own special recipe, which, of course, was my favorite. "What's the secret ingredient that makes it so good?"

"Oh, I add a bunch of this and that... and some herbs from the garden," he smiled as he handed me a big cup of soup with a slice of bread.

What that meant, I wasn't sure. But it tasted delicious, made for royalty. I finished every last drop of broth and patted my mouth with a napkin.

"Mmm, that's just what I needed! Your culinary creations are fit for a King!"

"Thank you! I'm glad you liked it," he grinned.

After taking the empty cup and spoon from me, he stopped and put his hand behind his ear.

"Listen Birdy... do you hear those two doves cooing?"

"What do you think they're saying?"

"I love you... I love you... I love you!"

"What a beautiful song... with words that never grow old."

"Birdy... *I love you!*"

"I believe it... you've shown me you do... in a million different ways."

"But... let me whisper it to your heart... once again!"

"I love you too... sooo much! Have I ever thanked you for being my perfect Gardener?"

"Yes," he grinned, "you've told me that at least seven times a day... every single day."

"I guess I have, but it just never seems to be enough."

"You can tell me for all eternity... I never tire of your love!" he replied with an extra tenderness in his voice. He then turned and looked deep into my eyes, "There is something very close to my heart I need to tell you as well. Do you know that you are my utmost delight? I gave everything I have for you... and I will always love you with a never-ending love!" Carefully choosing his words, he continued, "Birdy... today is an important day for us." Softening his voice to almost a whisper, he tenderly asked, "Will you trust me?"

"Why do you ask? Of course, I trust you!"

"Well... 70 years ago, you invited me into your garden. Now today, I would like to invite you to my garden."

His warm smile let me know I could rest in his perfect care. I sat silent for several moments, contemplating what he just said. I knew this day would eventually come. My eyes began to fill with tears, although I couldn't tell if they were happy or sad.

"I want to go... but I will miss those I love so much!"

"Your loved ones will soon follow, and we will be there together to greet them," he promised. "Besides, your dear mother will be waiting for you... and your dad will be there as well."

"Of course... for years I looked forward to seeing them again. I remember when you first told me she had a garden... but she never talked about it... she did take me there to visit on occasion though. It's the place she retreated to for peace and strength... you were there the whole time... weren't you?"

"Yes... indeed, I was," he warmly smiled, revealing his deep love for her. "I loved working in your mother's garden. She invited me to

be her Gardener at a very young age... and we spent many
wonderful years together... but life took her into uncharted waters,
full of droughts and storms. I never left her though. And now... she
is flourishing with abundant life in my garden."

"Do you think she will be surprised to see me?"

"Well, Birdy... I'm not sure if she'll be surprised... but I do know
she'll be overjoyed to see you. Before your mother came to live in
my garden, she asked me to take care of you, and I promised I
would."

"You kept your promise!" I exclaimed, now wiping tears of joy
from my eyes. "Oh, I miss her so much... but I'm going to see her
soon... and my dad too!"

The Gardener's eyes tenderly rested on mine while I cried and
laughed at the same time. Yes, I dreamed of this day my entire life,
and now the moment finally arrived.

"But what about my garden... I don't want to leave it here?"

"You don't have to worry my dear... it's coming with you! It will
become part of my glorious garden!"

"Oh how wonderful!" I clapped my hands together and laughed.
"It's my homecoming... and I'm ready to go!"

I sat silently for a while, staring at the canvas of radiant autumn
leaves adorning the ground.

"What are you thinking about?" the Gardener asked, bringing my
thoughts back to our beautiful afternoon.

Before I could answer, he reached behind the bench and handed
me a big bouquet of snow-white daisies with sunny yellow centers.

"These are for you my love... Happy 70th Anniversary! I grew
them in the greenhouse just for you... and you certainly deserve
them," he whispered, giving me a proud smile.

"They're stunning! Thank you so much... I feel extra cherished!
You already gave me this beautiful rose, but... you know daisies are
my favorite... don't you?"

"I do... and each flower has a message for you."

"Yes... but I'm going to leave all the petals on, and not even ask if
'He loves me or loves me not.'"

"And why is that my dear?"

"Because I know 'He loves me'... and I have never forgotten it!"

"Do you remember years ago in your mother's garden, when I told you that all daisy petals say, 'He always loves you... and you must never forget it'?"

"I remember it like yesterday... I wanted to hide when you caught me picking that flower... I thought you would scold me. But instead, you told me I was loved. You have proved it over and over again... nothing means more to me in the entire world than to be loved by you!"

"I loved you then as much as I love you now!" His eyes beamed with radiant joy, "That little eight-year-old has learned the meaning of love. Now she is a beautiful example of that very love, touching the lives of everyone she meets!"

"*Your* love is the essence of my garden... and my love is but a shadow of yours," I responded, not quite sure what to say since I never accepted compliments very well.

The Gardener understood this and simply smiled back. As I leaned on him, an indescribable peace enveloped me, carefully lifting me in my fragile moment. I could trust his impeccable timing with every second of my life. Even now, his comfort quieted me with sweet tranquility. The fear of death no longer gripped me because I knew my life would not end in terror, nor would I return to dirt. I knew I was more than dirt! Many years ago, the Gardener buried his seed in the earth, but it could not stay dead. It triumphantly burst forth with resurrected life and conquered death once and for all. This is the same immortal seed he planted in my garden. Now I cannot die. Soon he will take me to his garden where I will flourish in his presence for all eternity.

I slowly gazed over my garden, enjoying the serene stillness. The last of the day's sunshine glistened through the remaining golden leaves dangling from the trees. One by one, they fluttered to the ground leaving rich memories of a fruitful life. It reminded me of the many autumn harvests we enjoyed together. When I glanced at the Gardener, I found him tenderly watching me with the same sensitive care he gave the garden throughout the years.

"How faithful you have always been to me," I faintly whispered.

He smiled affectionately and took my hand in his. We lingered quietly for what seemed like minutes, but in reality, could've been hours. Perfect love radiated from his eyes, drawing my reflections into sweet unity with his heart. He knew my thoughts, and I knew his. He said nothing and I said nothing, yet we communicated in the most precious way about the most profound things. The beautiful silence ordained for this very moment expressed the years of friendship we shared.

Carefully placing his arm around my back, he drew me even closer to himself. Then closing my eyes, I rested my head on his chest as his strong arms held my body.

Like a father cradling his child to sleep with a lullaby, he began to hum ever-so-softly. As I breathed in my last breath, I savored his familiar heavenly scent I had grown to know and love over the years. Humming softer still, the Gardener hushed his sweet song into perfect silence. Then placing his lips on my forehead, he sealed me with a tender kiss that lovingly put my soul to rest.

My garden slept in peace.

All laid silent as he gently carried me home to his garden.

~ *"…nothing means more to me in the entire world*

than to be loved by you!" ~

Epilogue

A warm wave of light awakened me to a new beginning. Once again, I found myself in the arms of my beloved Gardener. His overwhelming love embraced my soul with hallowed peace. Only a faint memory of dirt lingered, reminding me of the flourishing bouquet of life I had become in the Master's hands.

"Is... this... your garden?"

A crystal stream bubbled past me, leaving waterfalls in its path. Trees and flowers burst forth with beautiful colors I'd never seen before. Animals scampered about and children played while a soft anthem of praise filled the air. My awestruck eyes beheld a never-ending rainbow crowning the glorious landscape. And just as the Gardener promised, the treasured faces of my precious mom and dad awaited me, making the garden's splendor all the more brilliant.

"It's majestic... so majestic... every part emanates your love! Am I dreaming?"

I reached out and touched his scarred brow.

He was real, *very* real! Tears of inexpressible joy rolled down my cheeks. He gently wiped them away with his nail-pierced hands, like he had done so many times before.

Then capturing my gaze with the usual twinkle in his eyes that greeted me every morning of my life, he leaned in closer and softly whispered, "Birdy... welcome home!"

"Forever... here with you... my Gardener?"

"Yes, my dear child... this blessed assurance is your divine destiny... for eternity!"

"I'm... I'm finally home."

"You are, my love... you are!"

For the LORD shall comfort Zion;
He will comfort all her waste places; and He will
make her wilderness like Eden, and her desert like
the garden of the LORD; joy and gladness shall be
found therein, thanksgiving, and the voice of melody.
Isaiah 51:3

Thou shalt no more be termed Forsaken; neither shall
thy land any more be termed Desolate: but thou shalt
be called Hephzibah, and thy land Beulah: for the
LORD delighteth in thee...
Isaiah 62:4

...the planting of the LORD,
that He might be glorified.
Isaiah 61:3

KJV

"Holiness

~as I then wrote down some of my

contemplations on it~

appeared to me to be of a sweet, calm, pleasant,

charming, serene nature, which brought an

inexpressible purity, brightness, peacefulness,

ravishment to the soul; in other words,

that it made the soul like a field or garden

of God, with all manner of pleasant fruits and

flowers, all delightful and undisturbed,

enjoying a sweet calm and the gentle

vivifying beams of the sun."

~Jonathan Edwards

Garden Song

Invite me into Your garden Lord
Let me meet with You face to face,
Where all else pales in Your beauty Lord
Let me bask in Your perfect grace.

Open Your garden's gate for me
Let Your presence meet my gaze,
May I glean from Your faithful hope and truth
Teach me all Your ways.

Hide me in Your garden Lord
Bid me rest in Your sweet solace,
Safe in Your precious promises
At peace in Your arms' embrace.

Here with You in Your shelter's care
Your paradise of love,
Songs of joy from creation flow
Join heaven's chorus above.

The birds, the flowers, the trees declare
Your glorious Majesty,
While your cross, Your blood, Your life reveal
My glorious destiny.

There is more and more and more to know
To expect and expect some more,
Your never-ending supply of love
Abounding from heaven's bright shores.

Let me dwell with You in Your garden Lord
May I never leave Your side,
Let my ears ever hear Your tender voice
In Your secret place to abide.

Made in the USA
Middletown, DE
11 December 2023

45211038R00137